TROUBLE
with a
CAPITAL O

TROUBLE
with a
CAPITAL O

By Miss O, with
Devra Newberger Speregen

Illustrated by Hermine Brindak

Watson-Guptill Publications/New York

For Halle and her Peeps

Senior Editors: Jacqueline Ching & Julie Mazur
Project Editor: Cathy Hennessy
Production Manager: Joseph Illidge

First published in 2006 by Watson-Guptill Publications,
a division of VNU Business Media, Inc.,
770 Broadway, New York, NY 10003
www.wgpub.com

Library of Congress Cataloging-in-Publication Data

Speregen, Devra Newberger.
  Trouble with a capital O / by Miss O ; with Devra Newberger Speregen ; illustrated by
Hermine Brindak.
      p. cm.
  Summary: Saddled with "the meanest teacher in the whole school" and a suddenly distant
older sister, fifth-grader Olivia, nicknamed Miss O, finds enjoyment playing soccer, baking
fabulous desserts, and being with her best friends.
  ISBN-13: 978-0-8230-2946-4 (alk. paper)
  ISBN-10: 0-8230-2946-8 (alk. paper)
  [1. Teachers--Fiction. 2. Schools--Fiction. 3. Sisters--Fiction. 4. Best friends--Fiction. 5.
Friendship--Fiction.] I. Brindak, Hermine, ill. II. Title.
  PZ7.S7489Tr 2006
  [Fic]--dc22
                              2006007516

Printed in the U.S.A.
First printing, 2006

Contents

juliette isabella miss O harlie justine

Meet the group!

Welcome to
Miss O and Friends!

When I, the real Juliette, was ten years old, I created the basis for Miss O and Friends. It all started when I was on the way home from a family vacation. I was bored, so I tried to think of something fun to do. The only thing that I could really do was draw. I borrowed some paper from my mom and started to draw "cool girls." I gave them to my mom and, like all mothers, she told me they were nice and put them in her purse. Little did she know that one day these drawings would turn into something much bigger.

Years later, with the help of my mom, my sister, and some friends, we started to create the Miss O girls. At first, it was just something fun to do—we'd play around on the computer creating all sorts of stuff. It wasn't until we realized that girls really liked our characters that the idea came to us to start a company. Now, thanks to girls like you, the Miss O & Friends website (www.missoandfriends.com) has become the most popular tween site ever!

The five Miss O girls are based on girls just like you and me, and they all possess important values and do things they love to do. This new book series features a story from each of the girls. Miss O narrates this book—the very first one in the series. We hope you enjoy it!

Chapter 1
First Day Freak Out

On the first day of fifth grade I woke up to a loud scream.

I bolted up from my comfy, warm bed, knocking my pillow to the floor. "Huh? What's going on?" I said groggily, scanning my room for signs of someone in trouble. "Who's there?"

I rubbed the sleep from my eyes and focused on the alarm clock. Six a.m.! Darn. I'd still had another fifteen minutes of sleep left. Then I heard the loud scream again.

Aaaaaahhhhhhhh!

But this time, I didn't jump. Or even flinch. Awake now, I knew exactly what was going on. With a big yawn, I walked over to my computer and tapped the mouse so the screen would light up. When it did, I saw the familiar IM box from my older sister Juliette. She was instant messaging me from her bedroom. Next door.

JUJEbee1: Miss O what r u wearing??!! :o

I had to laugh. We'd spent a whole two hours last night picking out our first day outfits!

gOalgirl: same thing we picked out last nite!
tie-dye skirt & tank!
JUJEbee1: PLS PLS come HELP ME!! PLS!!!
gOalgirl: OK, OK. B rite there.

I found my sister standing in the middle of her bedroom, surrounded by almost every piece of clothing she owned.

"Juje!" I cried. (That's what I call my sister—pronounced *Joo-Jee*—when I'm feeling extra sister-ish.)

"What happened to the capris and tank we picked out last night? You looked so awesome in that!" I told her. I gazed around her room in complete amazement. She had totally emptied her drawers onto her carpet. Usually she was a neat freak, so it was pretty weird to see her room all a mess.

Juliette frowned. "I was going to wear that, I swear!" she replied. "But then last night I started thinking, what if nobody in sixth wears capris on the first day of middle division? Then I'd look like a freak!"

I fell onto Juliette's bed and pulled my messy, just-woke-up hair out of my eyes and back into a pony. I always keep an elastic around my wrist, so I can make a pony whenever I want. Yes, I even sleep with one on my wrist! I pulled the day-glo green band off my arm and wrapped it around my hair.

"I mean it, Miss O," Juliette went on. (My nickname is Miss O. It's short for "Olivia." Dad called me Miss O when I was little and it just sort of stuck.)

"I barely slept all night because I was so freaked about school today," Juliette yawned. "What if my outfit is all wrong? What if I get lost in the new building? What if I'm not in classes with anyone I know?"

I groaned loudly. "You think *you've* got problems?" I asked as I made a near-perfect pony. "I wish my biggest concern today was whether or not to wear capris!"

My sister stopped freaking out and sat down on her bed next to me. "Wow, you're right," she said sympathetically. "I'm sorry, Miss O! Here I am going all psycho on you, when you've got just one hour left until the Hinter Monster."

I let out a deep sigh. "Yup. The Hinter Monster," I repeated. "What am I going to do?"

Actually, my new teacher's name was Mrs. Hintermeister, but for as long as I've been going to the Sage School, she's been known as "The Hinter Monster." And boy, is she awful! Juliette told me she's the meanest teacher in the school and she yells a lot. Plus, she leaves kids back a grade all the time! Juliette also told me she once heard a rumor that the Hinter Monster threw chalk at a student and hit him in the eye. The poor kid needed eye surgery after that! Can you believe it?

So, yes, I felt sorry for Juliette and her big outfit dilemma. But my problems were definitely a whole lot bigger at the moment.

I got up from Juliette's bed and made my way across the room to where a big pile of her jeans sat on the floor. Pairs of jeans shorts, jeans skirts, and jeans capris were in a big heap. Mom was going to freak when she saw that.

Me? I hardly ever wear jeans. But Juliette wears them all the time. I prefer sporty clothes like Soffes and tie-dyes.

"Here," I said, tossing Juliette a jeans skort. "Dilemma solved. Now back to my problems."

Just then, a loud "*Moo!*" filled the room. Juliette and I exchanged looks.

"Isabella!" we both said at the same time. I leaned over Juliette's computer to find a new IM box open. It was a message from one of our best friends, Isabella. She had picked a cow mooing as her IM buddy sound. It sounded so funny whenever she IM'd us. Despite my lousy mood this morning, I still chuckled when I heard it.

IzzyBELLA: HEY guys! R U there??? :)

I typed back to her.

JUJEbee1: Hi, Isabella. It's me, Miss O. I'm in
Juliette's room helping her find an outfit.
IzzyBELLA: HUH????? Thought capris/tank?
JUJEbee1: Nope. She changed mind. What about U?
IzzyBELLA: Soffes & b-ball jersey.

I smiled to myself. Did I even have to ask? That was Izzy's favorite outfit. She collects basketball jerseys and wears a different one every day. Isabella loves everything about basketball: watching it, playing it, even reading about it. She's my only friend who reads the entire sports section of the newspaper every single day.

Before I could reply to Isabella, another IM box appeared, this time the sound of a cash register filled the air. That was Harlie, another one of our friends.

harliegirl95: Hey, Juliette! Where's Miss O? Been
trying 2 IM her but she isn't answer-
ing. She OK???
JUJEbee1: Hi, Harl. It's me, Miss O. I'm in Juliette's
room.

harliegirl95: U OK?
JUJEbee1: NO!!!!!!!!
harliegirl95: bc of THM?
JUJUbee1: yes. :(
harliegirl95: I feel SO bad 4 U! :(

My sister read the IMs over my shoulder. "So Justine isn't awake yet?" she joked, noticing our other best bud hadn't joined in on the conversation yet.

Wouldn't you know it, just then we heard a loud door opening—the sound of someone signing onto Juliette's buddy list. It was Justine!

justME713: Hey, Juliette where's Miss O?

Juliette pushed me away from the keyboard and her fingers flew over the keys.

JUJEbee1: lemme get U all caught up: I changed
my outfit & Miss O is still freaking out
bc of THM. :O
justME713: UGH. tell Miss O I feel so bad 4 her!
anything I can do????
JUJEbee1: yes – tell girlz 2 meet @ doorz b4 class.
justME713: got it. Doorz. Cul8r.

The "doorz" were the double doors at the school entrance by the gym, where we all liked to meet in the mornings before class started. You know, just to say, "Hey," and to catch up on whatever from the night before. I was glad Juliette had asked everyone to meet there this morning. I needed my peeps big time!

Juliette signed off, then looked at the clock. "Ack! It's getting late," she shrieked. "Mom will be in any minute!"

Mom usually popped her head in our bedroom doorways in the morning to tell us to hurry up and get ready for the walk to school.

Juliette and I go to a private school just two blocks from our house in Westchester, New York. Mom and Dad have been letting us walk together to school by ourselves since last year. We love walking to school. Juliette always jokes that we're just too cool for the bus!

Isabella lives on the same block as us, so she walks with us, too. Justine lives in another town, so she rides the school bus. Harlie lives in New York City and has to first take a city bus, and then a school bus, so she has the longest ride of all. We're all starting fifth grade this year, except for Juliette, who is starting sixth.

At the Sage School, sixth, seventh, and eighth grades are all in a brand new building next to our building. I was excited for Juliette—middle division was a really big deal! So I understood why she was anxious about her outfit. But I also knew that whatever she wore, she was going to look great.

As for me, there was no way to fix my problem. I had been assigned to the Hinter Monster's class and there wasn't a darn thing I could do about it. I was looking at ten months of torture. I suddenly wondered if I should ask my mom to get me glasses. My eyesight was fine, but glasses would protect my eyes from flying chalk.

Juliette gave me a concerned look. "Let's go get you ready." she said. "Just try and stop thinking about the Hinter Monster. There's nothing you can do about it. Did you get any sleep last night?" she asked.

"No," I told her. "All I could think about was how horrible fifth grade was going to be. Why did I have to get the worst teacher in the whole school?"

I watched Juliette match her skort to a dark blue t-shirt with an electric guitar on the front. She turned to model her outfit for me. "How's this look?" she asked.

"Very cool," I said, meaning it. That dark blue T-shirt of hers was my fave. I had borrowed it many times before—it was one of the few items of clothing we both liked and shared. We may be sisters, but we have very different styles.

Watching Juliette get ready, I suddenly realized that school was going to be way weird without her this year. I mean, I know *technically* we'll still be at the same school. But middle division is in another building. It's not like I was going see her in the hallways, or get to sit with her in the cafeteria like we always did. Thinking about it made my stomach uneasy. How was I going to get through the Hinter Monster's class every day, without Juliette around for support?

I cleared my throat and made my way to the bedroom door. I have to be honest with you, I suddenly felt like crying. That's how bad I was feeling. It was going to be a long day. Scratch that—it was going to be a long *year*.

Juliette followed me into my room, which, though not nearly as bad as her's at the moment, was still pretty messy. Actually that's the way I like it. I have a system: I keep my fave clothes on *top* of my dresser, this way I can "see" what is clean and available to wear. I mean, if it's hidden in my drawer, how am I supposed to know it's there?

Of course, Mom hates my "system." She's always begging me to put my clothes away.

As I got ready, Juliette reminded me that although Mrs. Hintermeister was known as a yeller, she wasn't really the *worst* teacher in school.

"There are lots of teachers that are much worse," she said.

"I guess," I muttered as I pulled on my Soffe shorts. "But Hintermeister's the worst in lower division," I pointed out. "And lucky me! I got her!"

"Well, I think you'll be fine," Juliette said matter-of-factly. "Just try to stop being nervous. Maybe the Hinter Monster will *like* you! Maybe you'll be the teacher's pet!"

"Yeah, sure," I said with a snort. "Really, Juliette," I added in all seriousness. "Maybe you can help me think of a way to get transferred out of the Hinter Monster's class?"

Juliette shook her head and I sighed, knowing *that* would be next to impossible. At the Sage School, switching classes was never an option. Especially if your only reason for wanting to switch was that your teacher yelled a lot and gave a ton of homework.

Just then, Mom stuck her head in the doorway. "Olivia, put your clothes away," she said.

"Yeah, yeah," I muttered.

"And Juliette," she asked. "What happened to your room?"

"Sorry, Mom!" Juliette replied. "I know it's a disaster. I'll clean it up when I get home. I promise!"

Mom made a face. "Okay," she said. "But I'm trusting you to keep your word! Now you had both better hurry up. You still need to eat breakfast and wash up before we leave. Come on, girls, smile! It's the first day of school! Aren't you excited?"

Juliette and I looked at each other.

"Not really," we both answered at the same exact time.

Chapter 2
The Hinter Monster

Harlie and Justine were waiting for us at the "doorz," just as we'd planned. Isabella, Juliette, and I said good-bye to our moms, then hurried over to meet our friends.

"Harlie, you got a haircut!" Juliette cried out. "It looks *so* great!"

Harlie's hair really did look great. She wears it in a very short style, and though she never ever brushes it, it always falls into place perfectly. Her new haircut had wispy bangs.

"Yeah, great cut!" I told her. "And look, Justine, we have almost the same backpack!" Everyone stopped to check out our bags. I had chosen a different kind of schoolbag this year. Instead of the usual backpack style, I'd convinced my parents to buy me a messenger-style bag. I liked wearing it over my head and over one shoulder so the bag part hung to the side. It was two shades of blue and very cool. Justine had almost the same exact one in brown.

Although we're the bestest of friends, Justine and I are very different. She's worldy, which means she knows a lot about the rest of the world. That comes from having lived in so many different places! Justine's father is in the United States Army, so her family has moved around a lot. They lived in England for a while, and in Germany. Justine can speak two other languages, too, which I think is awesome.

As for style, Justine has got a lot of it. She always wears the coolest, newest fashions but she never looks out of place or like she's trying too hard. She always looks great! She's real pretty, too, with long, long, curly hair and light brown skin. Oh, and another thing Justine and I have in common: We both love to make jewelry! Justine makes the most amazing jewelry. This morning she was wearing a wristwatch she'd decorated with ice blue gemstones.

"I want to iron patches all over my bag," Justine told us. "I was thinking maybe I would put flag patches from different countries all over it. I can do yours, too, Miss O. If you want."

I nodded. "That sounds cool. Thanks. But can we put soccer patches on mine? Like team patches from different countries?"

Justine grinned at me. "I think that would look so cool!" she said.

Harlie suddenly put her hand on my shoulder. "So how ya doin'?" she asked, her voice filled with concern.

"Not so great," I said. "Last night was the worst!! I kept dreaming I failed all my tests and got left back, while all you guys moved up to sixth!"

"Oh, come on, Miss O!" Isabella said, pushing her wavy brown hair away from her eyes. "That would never happen! You're too smart to fail all your tests!"

I noticed Isabella had finally convinced her mother to let her get highlights. Her hair looked so pretty!

"Really," Harlie added, "you'll be fine. Just lay low and keep on her good side. I hear she likes smart kids. So you'll be good to go!"

"Just be yourself," Justine added.

"Yeah, only don't be yourself *too much*!" Harlie said with a laugh.

"Huh?" I asked. "What's that supposed to mean?"

Harlie bit her bottom lip. "No! I didn't mean that in a bad way," she said. "Just don't be so . . . you know . . . *talkative*."

"Are you calling me high maintenance?" I asked.

Isabella stepped in. "What Harlie means," she said diplomatically, "is that you tend to be a little *enthusiastic*. Take it down a notch," she offered. "Just so you won't stand out so much."

"So what you're saying is that I'm loud and obnoxious?" I asked.

"No!" they all cried out in unison.

"Okay, girlfriends," Juliette said, clearing her throat. "Time to change the subject!"

Harlie seemed relieved. "Good idea!"

"I hate to say this, chicas," Juliette went on, "but it's time for me to go! Please take care of my baby sister for me—even though she's being dramatic over this whole Hinter Monster thing."

"Hey! I'm not being dramatic!" I insisted.

Juliette's eyes widened. "So you're saying it was completely normal to ask Mom to get you glasses this morning?"

"Glasses?" Justine asked. "But you have perfect vision, Miss O."

"I know," I said, not liking where this was going.

"She told me glasses would protect her eyes . . . from flying chalk," Juliette explained.

The others burst out laughing.

"You're nuts, Miss O!" Harlie said.

"Really!" Isabella added.

I bit my bottom lip. "Okay, maybe I'm being a *little* dramatic. But it *could* happen!"

Juliette pulled on her backpack and fixed her hair.

"Okay. I'm off!" she said in a semi-nervous voice. "Wish me luck!"

We all made sad faces.

"I know! I know!" she said sweetly. "I'm going to miss you, too! It won't be the same in middle division, without you guys."

Isabella gave Juliette a hug, then Harlie and Justine did, too.

"We'll still see you for lunch, right?" Harlie asked. Both the lower division and middle division shared a cafeteria, but it was split into two cafeterias and the older kids always ate in one, while we ate in the other. I imagined Juliette would now be eating with the older kids.

"Definitely!" Juliette said to my surprise.

My eyes widened. "Really, Juliette?" I asked. "Cause that would be great. Especially today. I really need you there."

Juliette gave me a hug and I held on for a little longer maybe than I should have. There we were, having a dopey "sister moment," so it was really funny when Isabella said, "And I think I'll miss you most of all, Scarecrow!" as if we were acting out that scene from *The Wizard of Oz* where Dorothy says goodbye to the Scarecrow, the Lion, and the Tin Man.

We were all still laughing as we watched Juliette head toward her new building. Then the four of us turned to face our old building.

"I can't believe none of us are in the same class together," Justine remarked as we started walking toward the doors.

"I know! How insane is that?" Harlie asked. "There are only four fifth-grade classes, and we all ended up in a different one. I'm going to miss not being with you this year, Miss O. We had so much fun in Mr. Feuerzeig's class!"

I nodded. Fourth grade had been the best. But if there was anybody who was going to be doing a lot of missing this year, it was going to be me. After all, I had the worst teacher and nobody to go through it with. "I wish one of you were going to be with me this year," I said softly.

My friends all looked at me kind of strangely.

"Are you kidding?" Harlie said finally. "Sorry, Miss O. But, no way! I don't know what I would do if I had the Hinter Monster!"

"Yeah," Isabella agreed.

"Yeah, sorry, Miss O," Justine added. "No offense, but I wouldn't want to be in your class this year."

I frowned. "Great. Thanks, guys," I muttered. But I didn't really blame them. I wouldn't want to be in my class this year either.

Harlie tried her best to lighten the mood. "So what do you say we meet for lunch?" she said cheerfully. "Right after the bell, let's meet by the butterfly habitat, then grab our old table and talk about our classes."

The butterfly habitat was in the back of the cafeteria and it had a separate door to get into, but the wall separating it from the cafeteria was made of glass so you could see all the butterflies that lived inside while you ate lunch in the cafeteria. It was pretty cool.

"Okay," I said. "Butterfly habitat it is." I shot one last look at my best friends, then readjusted the strap of my bag. I felt like I was headed into battle or something. "See you later," I told them. Then I remembered the chalk-throwing teacher I was about to meet and added, "hopefully, I'll still have both my eyes."

As I headed toward my classroom, I thought about the Hinter Monster and wondered what she was really like. I mean, would the Sage School even let her teach if she was *that* horrible? If she screamed at kids all day and threw chalk at people . . . wouldn't she lose her job? Of course she would, I told myself. Mrs. Hintermeister really couldn't be *that* bad, I decided.

As soon as I stepped into my new classroom, I knew I was wrong. Yes, she *could* be that bad. In fact, she *was* that bad. I had barely taken three steps into the room, and already my new teacher was yelling. At the top of her lungs. I instantly froze.

Okay, maybe it wasn't exactly at the top of her lungs, but she was yelling at Cody Brooks for something, and her voice was definitely loud and angry.

"This behavior is unacceptable in my classroom!" Mrs. Hintermeister scolded. "Now put the desks back the way you found them and take your seats!"

I watched Cody and his friend Corey Greenberg push their desks to the back of the classroom.

"You, too, young lady," Mrs. Hintermeister said loudly. I turned to see who she was talking to this time, and I realized she was looking at me!

"Yes, I'm speaking to you," she said. "It's two minutes past eight and you are late for my class. I have a strict policy about lateness, and as soon as you find your seat, I'll explain how my consequences of lateness and misbehavior system works. Since it's the first day of school, you won't receive a consequences assignment. But please pay attention, so there won't be any further misunderstandings."

I had a lump stuck in my throat as I took a seat behind Lindsey Page, a girl I knew from soccer. She peered up at me as I slipped past her desk and I got the feeling she was really scared for me.

"Sorry," I mumbled, but I don't think Mrs. Hintermeister heard me. She was already in front of the room, explaining her code of conduct in the classroom. I noticed some kids had taken out their notebooks and were writing notes. I did the same. For the next twenty minutes, I wrote so much, my fingers ached.

As soon as she finished explaining the rules and the code and the consequences and the expectations, the Hinter Monster barely took a breath before beginning a math lesson! I couldn't believe it! We hadn't even unpacked our bags yet! She hadn't even asked us our names, or handed out our supply lists! And she for sure hadn't even made a "Welcome Back" speech like Mr. Feuerzeig had done last year. Here we were, 8:30 a.m. on the first day of school . . . already learning about fractions!

By the time lunch period rolled around, and I was copying the way-too-long homework assignment from the blackboard—in cursive!—I knew I wasn't going to last another minute, let alone an entire year, in the Hinter Monster's dungeon of dread.

Justine, Harlie, and Isabella were already waiting for me at the butterfly habitat when I got to the cafeteria. Isabella waved me over.

"Miss O! Over here! Hey, what's that in your hair?" she asked.

I put my hand up to touch my hair, just as Isabella let out a little giggle. "Is that a paper clip?" she asked.

My face turned red as I grumbled, "Yes." I pulled the paper clip out of my hair and stuffed it in my pocket. "Can we sit?" I asked.

"Uh, Miss O?" Harlie asked as she followed me to the table. "Aren't you going to tell us why you have paper clips in your hair?"

"It's just one, Harlie," I said.

"Okay, so what's it doing in your hair? Are you starting a funky, new hair jewelry line?"

"Ha-ha. No," I told them. "I just put it in my hair to hold back my bangs. The Hinter Monster made us take so many notes this morning and I couldn't see my paper because my bangs kept falling in my face. So I had to hold them back with a paper clip. Okay?"

Harlie made a face. "You had work today?" she asked.

"Yeah, didn't you?" I asked.

Harlie shook her head. "No, we played some name games so Miss Castrataro could learn all our names. No work."

"Mr. Kamin played his guitar for us!" Isabella gushed. "It was so cool! He's really good, you know."

I groaned. Great, it figures. I had the only teacher in the whole school who made her students do actual work on the first day of school.

"So, how'd it go?" Justine asked me. "Was it as bad as you thought?"

I nodded. "It was worse than bad," I told them. "Horrible."

"Did she throw chalk?" Harlie wanted to know.

I shook my head. "No. But she yelled a lot," I said. "Well, not really yelled," I added. "It's just kind of the way she talks. All the time. Her voice is loud and she always sounds angry." I had noticed that when we were going over the fractions worksheet. Mrs. Hintermeister's voice was always grumbly. She'd sounded as if she were mad at everyone—even the fractions!

"So what was the worst thing she did?" Justine asked as we took out our lunches.

I slumped in my chair. "She yelled at me for . . . *standing*," I replied.

Isabella's eyes widened. "For *standing*?" she asked.

"Yes. When I walked into the classroom, she was yelling at Cody Brooks, so I just stood there and then she started to yell at me for being late."

"You were late?" Justine asked.

"A minute late, I think."

Our table grew quiet. "Sounds terrible," Isabella said gently. "Sorry, Miss O. I wish you were in a different class."

I managed to smile. "Thanks, Isabella. Me, too." I sat upright in my chair and scanned the cafeteria. "Where's Juliette?" I asked the others.

Justine shrugged. "I don't know. She's not here yet. Should we wait for her to get here? I'm starving!"

"Nah. Let's start eating," I said. "I'd better not wait because if I take too long for lunch I might be ten seconds late for class. And then I'd be in danger of violating expectation number three of the Hinter Monster's code of conduct in the classroom and subject to section seven of the consequences of tardiness." I took a bite of my chicken salad sandwich.

"Huh?" Isabella asked.

When I looked up from my sandwich my three BFFs were staring at me in confusion.

I sighed. "Never mind," I told them. "I just don't want to be late."

Chapter 3
Isabella Goes Googling

The next morning, I knocked on Juliette's bedroom door to see about borrowing her slip-on running shoes. I had barely seen my sister yesterday after school because when she got home she had closed herself up in her room and hung her "Do NOT Under Any Circumstances Come In!" sign on her doorknob. I kind of had the feeling something was wrong, but I had so much homework last night (Yes! Homework on the first day!) I didn't really get the chance to talk to her about it. Plus, although she's the ultimate awesome sister, she can be kind of moody sometimes.

She didn't answer me when I knocked, so I knocked again. "Juliette?" I called out. "Can I come in?"

Juliette finally opened the door for me then went back to her computer. She was in the middle of an IM conversation with somebody who had a baby crying as her buddy sound. It was sort of funny to hear, "*Waah! Waah!*" coming from my sister's computer, especially because Juliette had recently changed her buddy sound to a great big hiccup.

"What's up?" she asked me as she typed.

"Oh, um, can I borrow your Nikes?" I asked.

"Yeah, whatever," Juliette replied. She continued to type.

"*Hiccup!*"

"*Waah! Waah!*"

I searched her closet for the sneakers until I found them under a pile of blankets and pillows on the floor. I turned to go, but stopped in the doorway.

"Who are you chatting with?" I asked.

"No one," she replied without turning away from the screen.

"No one?" I asked.

"Well, you don't know her," Juliette said as she typed.

"Oh," I said hesitantly. "Okay then. Um, by the way, we were waiting for you at lunch yesterday. How come you didn't show up?"

Finally, my sister turned around. "I just had a lot to do, that's all," she said. "And I didn't feel like walking *all the way* to the other cafeteria."

"*Waah! Waah!*" Juliette's new friend called out.

She turned around to reply and left me standing there in her doorway.

"Okay, whatever," I said. To be honest with you, I was more than a little annoyed. *All the way* to the other cafeteria? I thought to myself. It wasn't as if we were eating lunch in France! I mean, really.

I left her room, closing the door behind me. I could take a hint.

Back in my room, I finished getting dressed. Today was a gym day, so I was glad to able to dress as sporty as I liked. Luckily, it was still warm out, too, so I could wear shorts and my absolute favorite Manchester United

23 T-shirt. Twenty-three is Beckham's number. Beckham is David Beckham, the coolest soccer player in the world!

I don't know if I mentioned it already, but you should know that I am the biggest soccer fan on the planet. When I'm not playing in soccer games on Sundays, I love to watch World Cup Soccer on TV. Did you know soccer is called football in other countries? Isabella says it's called "futbol" in Peru, where she comes from originally.

I play center on my soccer team, the Wildcats, and last spring I had a great season! I scored eleven goals and had seventeen assists in total. At the end of the season, my whole team got trophies for coming in first place, and I got a patch for being the highest scorer. My dad sewed the patch onto my jersey for me and it looks really cool.

Anyway, today I was wearing my Manchester United T-shirt. That's the name of Beckham's former team in Great Britain. Now he plays for Real Madrid in Spain. Justine bought it for me when her family went to England for the summer. Wasn't that so nice of her? I love this shirt, and I'm always begging my parents to wash it so I can wear again.

I was pulling on my socks when I heard a loud "Moo!" Isabella was calling to me with an IM. At the same moment, my mom appeared in my doorway with some clean, folded laundry for me to put away.

"Was that a cow?" she asked in confusion.

I giggled. "Yeah, that's Isabella's IM," I told her.

"*Moo! Moo!*" We heard again.

My mother laughed. "Well you had better answer her," she said, "or she'll have a cow!"

"That's funny, Mom!" I said with a smile. "I'm going to tell her that!"

Laughing at her own joke, my mother put the pile of clothing on my dresser and left the room. I made my way over to my desk and tapped the mouse. This is what I saw when the screen lit up:

IzzyBELLA: Miss O!!! R U THERE???????
IzzyBELLA: Miss O!!! WHERE R U??????
IzzyBELLA: OMG, Miss O! I have to tell u something! Something HUGE!!! Miss O???

Sheesh! She was having a cow! I sat down at my desk and began to type.

gOalgirl: Yes! I'm here! Wassup, Izzy?
IzzyBELLA: FINALLY! I thought maybe u left already
and I wanted to make sure I caught
u b4 u did bc I
gOalgirl: OMG, Izzy! Get 2 the point!
IzzyBELLA: :) sorry! :) can't walk to school
2day...backpack WAY 2 heavy!!!
Wanna ride?
gOalgirl: THAT's the emergency???
IzzyBELLA: NO. MUST show U what I found!
gOalgirl: U can't tell me now???
IzzyBELLA: NO – have to SHOW U. Tell
Har/Juliette/Just, 2 meet us at doorz!
Will pick u up in 45 min
gOalgirl: OK. Doorz. Got it. C U in 45

I sent a quick IM to Harlie and Justine about meeting at the "doorz" before school, then I went back to Juliette's room to fill her in on the plan. I was sure she'd want a ride to school today, too, because thanks to all of the Sage School getting their school supply lists yesterday, everyone's backpack was probably stuffed to capacity.

I knocked, twice, but Juliette didn't answer. So I let myself in.

"Juliette?" I said, stepping into her room. "Isabella's mom is driving—" I stopped, because I was talking to an empty room.

Making my way downstairs to the kitchen, I called out to my sister. "Juliette!"

Mom stopped me at the bottom of the stairs. "Juliette left already," she told me.

"She did?" I asked in confusion. "She walked by herself?"

Mom shook her head. "No, honey. She got a ride from her friend Skyler."

"Really?" I asked. Well, I knew my mother wouldn't make up that story, but I said, "Really?" anyway. I couldn't believe Juliette would get a ride to school and not tell me about it or ask me if I wanted to go, too.

"Really," Mom replied. "I'll drive you if you want."

"That's okay," I told her. "Isabella's mom is going to give me a lift. But thanks."

"Good. So go grab a bite to eat before you leave," Mom said. I wasn't hungry at all, but I knew there was no use arguing with her about it. Mom has this thing about skipping breakfast.

A few minutes later, I heard Isabella's car horn. I gulped down the last of my cereal, then headed for the hall closet where I keep my book bag. I bent down to pick it up and practically pulled my shoulder muscle trying to lift it! The Hinter Monster had requested more school supplies than any other teacher, and last night Dad and I had practically cleaned out Staples buying everything on the list. I'd actually had to pack *two* book bags to bring to school today—my messenger bag, and an old backpack I had from last year—just to carry it all!

I gave Mom a quick kiss on the cheek, then managed to drag both bags out to Isabella's SUV. Both she and her mom were laughing as I stepped up into the truck.

"Well, if I'd known how much stuff you had," Isabella's mom joked, "I would have taken the bigger truck!"

"What's with the *ginormous* school supply collection?" Isabella asked, eyeing my two stuffed bags.

"Hintermeister," I grumbled, settling into my seat.

Isabella whistled. "Wow. What's in there?" she asked.

I tried to remember all the stuff my dad and I had bought last night. "Um, three-ring binders, black-and-white notebooks, book covers, a dictionary, spiral notebooks, twelve folders, crayons, markers, scissors, a hole punch, a calculator, reinforcements—"

"Reinforcements?" Isabella interrupted. "What are those?"

"I'm not sure," I told her. "But my dad said we got 'em."

Isabella laughed. "Where's Juliette?" she asked.

"Oh, she got a ride already," I told her.

Isabella made a face. "She did? With who?"

"With *whom*," her mother corrected from the front seat. Isabella's mom was really strict about speaking proper English. Probably because she grew up in Peru and when she moved here, she didn't know *any* English. Now she is an ESL tutor. ESL stands for "English as a Second Language."

"So, Izzy, what did you want to show—" I started to ask, but I noticed Isabella's eyes widen and she shook her head back and forth really quickly. I think she didn't want me to bring up her huge news in the car with her mom there.

"Show what, dear?" Isabella's mom asked from the front of the truck.

"Uh, show . . . show . . . show-and-tell!" I said finally, saying the first thing I could think of.

"Show-and-tell?" her mom asked. "What about it?"

I looked helplessly at Isabella. "Um, nothing," I sputtered. "I was just, uh, wondering if Isabella's class was going to have show-and-tell this year."

"Isn't show-and-tell for younger children?" her mother asked.

"Um. Uh, I don't know," I replied. Luckily it was a short ride and we were just pulling up to the school so I could end the whole ridiculous conversation. "Thanks for the ride!" I said, hauling my bags of rocks, I mean school supplies, out of the truck.

Isabella jumped out the opposite door with her normal-supply-of-school-supplies stuffed backpack and blew her mother a kiss. "*Véale más adelante, Mamá!*"

"See you later, too, *mi amor!*" her mom replied.

As her mother pulled away from drop-off, Isabella shot me look. "Show-and-tell?" she asked with one eyebrow raised.

I'd always wanted to learn how to do that—raise one eyebrow. Isabella looks so cool when she does that! But it must be something only some people can do, because even though I practiced one day in front of the mirror, I couldn't do it at all.

Anyway, I shrugged, as best as a person who was carrying two heavy bags could shrug. "So sue me!" I exclaimed. "I didn't know what to say! How was I supposed to know your *huge* info was supposed to be a *huge* secret?"

Isabella laughed. "Never mind. It was funny! But let's go meet the others. We don't have much time!"

I followed Isabella past the front entrance to the school, past the line of buses dropping off kids, past the mobs of kids shoving each other to get inside the building, all the way to the double doors by the gym. Justine was already there waiting for us, and Harlie was just stepping off her bus as we passed.

"I got the message!" Harlie called out to us. "What's up, guys?"

"Yeah, what's the big news?" Justine asked. "Where's Juliette?"

"She got a ride with Skyler," I told them.

They all stared at me as if I'd just said she rode to school with Shrek.

"With who?" Harlie asked.

"Skyler who?" Justine asked.

I shrugged. "I don't know," I told them. "But I think her IM buddy sound is a baby crying."

Nobody said anything.

"That's not very helpful," Justine pointed out.

"I know," I said. "But I don't have the 411 on Skyler. Juliette was being very secretive this morning and I didn't even get a chance to talk to her."

"Secretive about what?" Isabella asked.

"I'm not sure," I said. "She was IM'ing someone and I asked her who it was and she told me I didn't know her. That's pretty much it," I added. "I didn't see her when she made the plans to get a ride, and she didn't ask me to go with, so . . ."

"So she's not coming?" Justine asked.

"Nope." I didn't know what else to tell the girls. I mean, I was sort of mad at Juliette for not asking me if I'd wanted a ride with her and her new friend and I didn't want to talk about it anymore.

"Well, did you ask her what happened yesterday?" Justine asked me. "How come she didn't meet us for lunch?"

"She told me she couldn't," I said, leaving out the obnoxious part about her not wanting to walk *all the way* to the other cafeteria. "Anyway, what's up Isabella?" I asked, trying to change the subject. "What's this HUGE secret news you have?"

Isabella seemed as if she'd almost forgotten why she'd called this big meeting, but she snapped back to reality instantly. "Right!" she said. "Okay, so you're totally not going to believe what I found online last night!"

We all watched as she put her backpack on the ground and zipped it open. She pulled out a sheet of paper and held it to her chest so we couldn't see it.

"But you can't tell anybody!" she added. "My mom and stepdad would freak if they knew I was up Googling last night."

"How come?" Harlie asked. "What's the big deal?"

"No big deal," Isabella said. "They just don't like me Googling when I'm online alone."

"Okay! We promise!" I said for the three of us. "What is it already?"

Isabella gave us a look, then slowly turned the paper to face us. I immediately noticed there was a big picture of my teacher, Mrs. Hintermeister, on the center of the page. It was definitely a picture from when she was younger, but make no mistake about it, it was the Hintermeister. And she was *smiling*!

I grabbed the paper from Isabella.

"Let me see that!" I said. Harlie and Justine crowded around me to get a better look.

"It's from an article on the Web," Isabella said. "But that's all that was there," she added. "I couldn't find the actual article, just the picture and . . . that headline."

That *headline* was exactly what I was staring at with my jaw wide open in shock. The first surprise may have been that the Hinter Monster had a smile across her usual sourpuss face. But the bigger surprise was what the headline above the photograph said. I read it out loud, in utter disbelief.

"Local Teacher Behind Bars!"

Now we were *all* standing with our jaws hanging open.

Chapter 4
Big News!

"Holy Moley!" Harlie cried, staring down at the photo.

"You can say *that* again," I said.

"Holy Moley!" Harlie repeated. "I can't believe the Hinter Monster was in *jail*!"

"Does it say anything else, Miss O?" Justine asked, peering over my shoulder.

"Nope. Nothing," I said. I gazed up at Isabella. "Was there anything else? Any more information? *Anything*?"

"Uh-uh," Isabella said, shaking her head. "I couldn't find another word about it. And when I started to dig a little deeper, I heard my mom coming down the hallway so I shut off my computer. She hates when I stay up late and play games on the computer and stuff. And she especially hates the whole Googling thing. But I was just messing around, and I really wanted to see if that chalk story was for real. So I put 'Hintermeister' into the Google search bar, hit search, and, like, a million Hintermeister links popped up!"

"Wow! There are that many Hintermeisters?" Harlie asked.

Isabella nodded. "Yup. I didn't want to look through all of them, so I just saw one that said 'teacher' in it, and I clicked that one. That's when this photo appeared."

Justine suddenly nudged me in my arm. "Yikes! Look! The last bus is pulling away! Come on, we don't want to be late!"

Oh, no! I felt myself panic. I most certainly did not want to be late to class—for the second time in two days! I thrust the paper back to Isabella, threw my extremely heavy bags over my shoulders and raced as best I could toward the double doors.

"Lunch!" I yelled over my shoulder at the girls.

Making my way through the gym—half running, half waddling—I nearly crashed into Miss Jivin, the gym teacher.

"Sorry, Miss Jivin!" I apologized.

"No problem, Miss O," she said. "Just slow down!"

Can't slow down, I told myself, trying to move a little faster. How could I have let it get so late? *So much for my plan to be the first one in my seat this morning.*

If you think it's easy running through the hallways with two incredibly heavy bags of school supplies over your shoulders, I can assure you that it's *not*. In fact, it was next to impossible! My arms felt like they were going to fall off. It was probably those darn reinforcements—whatever they were—weighing me down!

I managed to catch a glimpse of a wall clock as I ran past one of the classrooms. I noticed I had less than a minute before the bell rang for class. And there was just one hallway left for me to navigate before it did. *Hey, maybe I can make it after all!*

One last hallway filled with kids stood between me and the dungeon of dread. I stared down the long corridor, toward my classroom at the very end, on the right. *Less than a minute . . . no problem.* I readjusted the bags' shoulder straps (which were digging into my skin something awful!), got into soccer-star mode, and I took off.

Funny, it was just like playing soccer, I thought, as I dodged past kids on my left and kids on my right. Gaining speed as I ran, I thought of my classroom as the goal zone, and I ticked down the game clock in my head as I moved.

Twenty . . . nineteen . . . eighteen . . .

"Oh! Hi, Mr. Feuerzeig!" I called out to my teacher from last year as I passed his classroom.

"Hi, Olivia!" he called back. "Please don't run in the halls!"

"Right! Okay!" I replied, slowing down a bit. I knew Mr. Feuerzeig would never get me in trouble though. He's one of the nicest teachers in the school!

Thirteen . . . twelve . . . eleven . . .

Ha! It was looking good! Then, all of a sudden . . .

"*Brrrrrriiinnnggg!*"

"Oh no!" I gasped! The bell!

I sprinted forward and stepped through the doorway, just as the bell stopped ringing. With a big grin and a big sigh of relief, I headed for my chair. *Goal!* I thought happily to myself.

"Olivia," Mrs. Hintermeister said loudly, interrupting my thoughts.

"Being on time for my class means being in your seat when the bell rings."

"But—"

"*In your seat,*" she repeated. "Not walking through the door, or sharpening your pencil, or throwing out trash," she went on. "In your seat."

"I'm, um, sorry, Mrs. Hintermeister," I grumbled. "But I had these heavy bags to carry and—"

"Please see my consequences chart for your punishment assignment," Mrs. Hintermeister said, not listening to my excuse at all. "It will be due first thing tomorrow morning. Please make sure you put it on my desk. Now, that's enough time spent on this interruption. Class, please take out your math textbooks and open to page twelve."

I fell into my chair with a groan—a quiet groan because I didn't want to break any more codes and receive any more consequence assignments. I have to tell you though, I was so mad! I sat there thinking some pretty nasty things about my teacher as I opened my bag to find my math textbook.

"Take out your homework assignments from last night," the Hinter Monster said, "and pass them up to the front of the class. Quietly."

I found my homework sheet and passed it to Lindsey who sat in front of me. "Does someone have the bathroom pass out?" I whispered to her as she reached for my homework sheet.

Lindsey's eyes grew wide with fear and she shushed me. Then she spun back around in her seat to face front and give Mrs. Hintermeister her full attention. It's really what I should have been doing at the moment, but wouldn't you know it . . . I *really* had to go to the bathroom!

"You're crazy if you ask for the pass!" Lindsey whispered back to me.

"Huh? Why?" I asked.

"*Duh*! Because you were just late!" she reminded me. "I heard she once punished a kid for being late and wouldn't let her have the bathroom pass. She made that kid wait so long for the pass, the kid ended up peeing in her pants!"

Oh, please. "Yeah, right," I muttered.

"No! Really!" Lindsey insisted.

True, this probably wasn't the best time to ask for the pass—having just been reprimanded and all—but I really had to go.

I sat back in frustration and crossed my legs. Would I be able to hold it in until gym? I wondered. I glanced at the clock. 8:07 a.m. Ugh. Just seven minutes have passed so far! Gym was still fifty-three minutes away. I didn't think I could make it that long, but Lindsey's story was going through my head. Why would she make it up? I wondered. Maybe if I—

"Olivia?" Mrs. Hintermeister's voice broke my train of thought.

"Yes?" I asked. My voice shook a little when I spoke, both from having to "go," and because I was nervous.

"I asked you for your answer to number seven. Will you please pay attention?"

I swallowed hard. "Yes," I replied.

The class was quiet. A few kids were staring at me, I noticed.

"Olivia?" Mrs. Hintermeister said again, sounding a little exasperated. "Number seven?"

"Oh! Right!" I managed to say. I shifted my eyes down to my textbook and figured out the answer to number seven. "One-half," I said.

"Correct," Mrs. Hintermeister replied.

Of course it's correct, I thought to myself. I've been an "A" math student since the first grade. It's my best subject!

Mrs. Hintermeister went on, quizzing us about our homework, and I sat in my chair, having to pee something *awful*. Without realizing it, I began shaking my leg.

Lindsey, however, totally noticed it. She turned slightly around in her chair and leaned all the way back in her chair to whisper harshly to me.

"Would you cut it out!" she said.

"Cut what out?" I asked.

"Stop shaking your leg like that! Your knee is hitting the back of my chair!"

"Well why don't you move your chair—" I started.

Before I could finish, Mrs. Hintermeister's voice interrupted me.

"Olivia and Lindsey!" she said sternly. "Do you know the consequence for talking while I'm talking?"

"I'm sorry, Mrs. Hintermeister!" Lindsey sputtered. "But Olivia is shaking her leg and it's right up against my chair and it's making my chair shake and my pencils keep rolling—"

"Olivia," Mrs. Hintermeister asked, "why are you bothering Lindsey?"

"No! I'm not!" I insisted. "I mean, I *am* bothering her, but not intentionally. I didn't notice my leg was shaking until she just asked me to stop."

Mrs. Hintermeister sighed in frustration. "Well, do you think you can manage to control yourself and your leg, Olivia?"

I cleared my throat. "Yes," I assured her. "But . . ." my voice trailed off. I needed that bathroom pass so bad! I could control my behavior and my leg, but I didn't think I could control *that* any longer!

"Yes?" Mrs. Hintermeister asked impatiently.

I couldn't do it.

"Never mind," I said quietly. Instead, I crossed my legs and prayed I would make it. I tried to think of other things. My first soccer game of the season on

Sunday, a good costume idea for Halloween, if Mom would let me have a sleepover this Saturday night—those sort of things. Then I thought about the photo of Mrs. Hintermeister that Isabella had found, and how the lady standing in the front of the classroom at that very moment was once a *criminal*!

Crazy, right? I mean, sure, she's the strictest teacher ever . . . but could the Hinter Monster really have spent time in prison?

I was lost in a daydream, picturing the Hinter Monster wearing black and white stripes and rattling a tin cup against the bars of a jail cell (I know, I watch way too many cartoons), when I heard everybody shutting their textbooks. Hooray! It was time for gym!

I raised my hand and asked for the bathroom pass.

"We're leaving for gym period in five minutes," Mrs. Hintermeister said. "Can you wait until then?"

"Not really," I said. "Please? It's an emergency!"

Mrs. Hintermeister frowned. "Fine. But please go quickly."

I leaped from my chair and unhooked the bathroom pass off the wall, then I flew out of the room. I couldn't believe I had waited like that all morning, just because I was afraid of my teacher. I really had to go! What if I had, you know, had an accident or something? Can you imagine how horrible that would have been?

And I think I read somewhere once that you should never, you know, hold it in for too long. That you can get an infection or something. I really hoped I hadn't gotten an infection. If I did, it would be the Hinter Monster's fault!

As I headed quickly down the hall toward the bathroom, all I could think about was that maybe the Hinter Monster *had* spent time behind bars. After all, she runs her classroom like a prison!

At lunchtime, I sat with Harlie, Justine, and Isabella. Again, Juliette was a no-show. Can you believe that? She was supposed to be our friend—*best friend*, I might add—she could at least have told us last night she wouldn't be eating with us anymore! I wanted to ask the girls how they felt about the situation, but at the moment, we were too busy discussing my teacher.

Isabella had spread out the picture of the Hinter Monster on the cafeteria table and we were all huddled over it.

"I can't believe she was a criminal," Isabella muttered, for, like, the hundredth time.

"Well, I can!" I grumbled. "You should see how she is in class!" I went on. "She's mean and strict and she makes you hold it in, even if you really have to go!"

Isabella ignored me. (Maybe because I had already told the story of having to hold it in three times.) "What I don't get," she said diplomatically, "is, if Mrs. Hintermeister was being sent to jail, why would she smile like that in the photo?"

We all inspected the photograph again.

"Maybe she was smiling *before* she knew she was going to jail?" Justine offered.

Harlie tapped her fork on her lunch tray. "Maybe," she said. "But that's not the face of someone who's about to go to jail."

"That's not even her face anymore," I pointed out. "She *never* smiles. Not once. The ends of her mouth are always pointed down in a frown, even when she's reading to herself." I had noticed this earlier, when we were taking turns reading from our literature anthology textbook.

"What I don't understand," Harlie went on, "is why the Sage School would hire a teacher who had been in jail. It doesn't make sense!"

"Do you think if we Google her again, we'll find out more information?" Justine wondered.

"I'm not allowed to Google," Isabella reminded us.

"I'm allowed to Google, but I have a gymnastics meet today after school," Harlie added.

"I never Googled a person before," I told them, "but I think it would be okay with my parents."

"Okay, but remember not to mention how you found this out!" Isabella said. "If your mom talks to my mom, I'll be in big trouble!"

"Don't worry," I said. "I won't. Maybe I'll ask Juliette to do it with me."

"Where is your sister anyway?" Harlie asked. "Doesn't she want to eat with us anymore?"

I shrugged. "Can I ask you guys something?"

"Sure. Shoot," Harlie said.

"It's about Juliette," I explained. I told them about how she had locked herself in her room when we got back from Staples last night, and how she barely even talked to me this morning in her room. And then about how she'd left for school with Skyler—without even telling me about it or asking me to go.

"Why don't you talk to her?" Isabella asked. "Just tell her you were wondering why she hasn't met us for lunch."

"I guess," I said. "I'll try to talk to her after school today. That is, if I can find a minute of freedom in between all the homework sheets and consequences assignments I have!"

"Oh, hey, that reminds me!" Isabella said excitedly. "Did you see the Sage Café bulletin board?"

I shook my head.

"Then you don't know about the Kids 'R Cookin' contest?"

"The what?" I asked.

"OMG! Come on! I'll show you. You're going to be so psyched!" Isabella picked up her tray and dumped out her trash. We were all finished with lunch, so we tossed out our garbage and followed Isabella to the bulletin board.

"I saw the flier when I came in," she said. "Check it out. You know the AH! Baked Goods Company? The one that makes those Magic Cookie Bars with the creamy peanut butter and chunks of milk chocolate and—"

"Wow, I *love* those!" Harlie gushed.

"Me, too!" I squealed. "I've been trying to figure out how they make those for years! Whenever I try to make them, the coconut and the chocolate bake at different times and the coconut burns and—"

Isabella rolled her eyes. "Will you be quiet and listen?" she asked.

"Right! Sorry!" I said. But once you get me talking about baking, I can go on and on for hours. Next to soccer, baking is my most favorite hobby in the world!

I started baking with my grandma Mimi when I was five years old. She showed me how to crack an egg without dropping the shells in the mixing bowl, and how to measure out different ingredients. Most of the things I know how to bake are Grandma Mimi's recipes, but sometimes I like to add something different or change an ingredient to make the recipe unique. My mom likes to bake, too, and lots of times we'll spend a Friday night together thinking up cool new recipes and testing them out.

"So anyway," Isabella went on, "the AH! Baked Goods Company is having a contest in schools all over New York. One kid from each school with the best dessert recipe will have his or her recipe entered in a second contest for all of New York State! And then the winner of *that* contest will get their recipe entered in a national contest!"

My eyes widened. "You mean our school is doing this?" I asked excitedly.

Isabella grinned. "Yup! It's next Friday. You have to come up with an original recipe, make it, and bring it in for the judges."

Harlie grabbed me by the shoulders. "Miss O!" she cried. "You can totally do this!"

"And win!" Justine piped in. "You're the best baker we know! Even better than a lot of our mothers!"

I was smiling from ear to ear, forgetting for a moment my problems with the Hinter Monster and with my sister. This was something I could get stoked about! I mean, I actually had a chance at winning this thing!

I suddenly found myself daydreaming, picturing myself winning the AH! Baked Goods contest at school. My friends were all there by my side, cheering me on. Then I pictured myself winning the New York State contest! And then the national contest! Then I imagined myself standing in the AH! Baked Goods factory, watching Miss O's Outrageous recipes being baked by the billions! Cookie and cake boxes with my picture on them were rolling off huge printing machines! The smell of chocolate and nutmeg was in the air!

"Miss O! Miss O!" the reporters all called out to me. "Can we take your picture? Here, hold up a box of your famous cookies!"

"*Brrrrrriiinnnggg!*"

Dang! The warning bell. Lunch was now officially over and class would begin again in five minutes.

"Miss O?" Isabella asked. "Which recipe are you going to enter?"

I bit my bottom lip. It was a tough decision, because I had so many great baking recipes to choose from. But then I had an idea.

"Tomorrow," I told my friends, "at lunch, I want you guys to vote on which recipe you think I should enter in the contest."

The girls all smiled.

"After all, this is like having a shot at becoming the next Mrs. Fields, or Keebler Elf, and I want all of you guys to have a piece of the action!"

"Sounds cool," Harlie said. "As long as we also get to have a piece of the winning recipe!" she added with a wink.

Chapter 5
My Sister, the Alien

After school, and after ten minutes of waiting for Juliette to see if she wanted to walk home with us, Isabella and I headed home without her. It was weird that she hadn't shown up.

Anyway, I had so much to do when I got home, I couldn't even think straight. What to do first, I wondered—my homework, my consequences assignment, or get my recipes together for the vote tomorrow? Obviously, my schoolwork was the most important, so I probably should start with that. I had so much of it, too! Three math sheets, a science vocabulary match-up, a map skills worksheet, and I had to study for a spelling quiz.

I kicked off my Nikes, grabbed a snack, then headed up to my room. As I walked past Juliette's door (which was closed) I could hear her inside on her computer. I rapped a few times on her door and waited for her to answer. I was dying to show her the picture of Mrs. Hintermeister that Isabella had found. I dropped my bag on the floor and pulled out the photograph.

"Juliette?" I called out, knocking again. Hmmm. This seems familiar, I said to myself. Right back to where I'd been that very morning . . . standing outside Juliette's door, waiting for her to let me come in.

"Juje?" I asked a third time. "It's me!"

"Okay, come in," Juliette finally called out.

I pushed open the door. "I have *got* to show you something!" I announced. "You are going to *freak out!*"

Juliette was IM'ing Miss "Waah Waah!" again, so I waited for her to turn around. When she didn't, I walked over to her desk.

My sister spun around in her chair. "This conversation is private!" she said to me, trying to cover the computer screen with her arm.

I stared at her in confusion. "Huh?"

"Private," she repeated.

I was so surprised to hear her say that, I kind of just stood there for a minute, not saying anything else. It wasn't like Juliette to be so secretive—especially around me! We usually told each other everything!

"Oh, sure. That's fine," I stammered. "I wasn't going to read it anyway. I just want to show you something."

Juliette snapped off her screen, then stood up to face me. "Okay, what?" she asked.

Wow, I thought. What was with the 'tude?

"What's the matter with you?" I asked.

"What do you mean?" she replied.

I stared at her, thinking that something seemed different about my sister lately. Ever since school had started. I couldn't explain it exactly, but the way she was talking to me, the way she was being all private and stuff, the way she was closing her door all the time . . . something was going on.

"I mean, are you mad at me for something?" I asked her. "You seem—I don't know—a little weird lately."

Juliette rolled her eyes at me. "No, I'm not mad."

"Then why are you acting so . . . so . . . "

"So *what*?" she asked.

"I don't know!" I answered. "Different, that's all."

"Miss O, I'm not mad! And I'm not acting different. I'm the same person I was. I'm just in the middle of something, so show me what you wanted to show me so I can get back to my conversation."

"Who are you talking to?" I asked. "Skyler?"

Juliette's eyes widened. "How do you know Skyler?" she asked.

"I don't know her," I said. "But mom told me you got a ride with her, so I thought maybe she was a new friend of yours."

"Okay, so it's Skyler. Satisfied?"

I made a face. "I really don't care, I just was wondering why you were being so secretive and all."

"Can you just get on with it?" Juliette asked in annoyance.

I couldn't believe how snippy my sister was being. Honestly, if I hadn't had the gossip item of the decade to show her, I would have just turned around and left her room. But I *had* to show her Isabella's picture of Mrs. Hintermeister. It was going to knock her socks off! I'll bet she would snap right out of her "obnoxiosity" (I know that's not a real word, but I made it up and I think it describes how Juliette's been acting perfectly!).

"Okay," I said. "But get ready for your eyes to pop out of your head and roll onto the floor!"

"Miss O–" my sister said with a sigh. "I mean really."

So I shoved the photograph under her nose and waited for her reaction.

Juliette's eyes narrowed as she looked closely at the photo, then as she read the headline. "Behind bars?" she asked. "What is this? This is stupid. Come on, Miss O, I was in the middle of an important conversation—"

Huh? Did she not get it?

"Juliette, did you read the headline?" I asked in amazement.

"Yes! I read it," she said. "So? You made a funny photo of your teacher on the computer. Big deal."

I couldn't believe what I was hearing. "No!" I exclaimed. "I didn't *make* this photo! Isabella found it online when she Googled Hintermeister!"

"Whatever," Juliette replied, flipping her computer screen back on. "I really have to finish this," she said, "so I can start my homework. You get a ton of homework in middle division, you know."

I just stared at her in disbelief. How was this possible? How could it be that she really couldn't care less about my *huge* news?

I spun around in frustration and left my sister's room, pulling her door closed behind me with a loud jerk. Fine! I thought. If she was going to be like that, then I would, too!

Fine!

As I made my way into my room and over to my desk, I tried to think if I had done or said anything during the past few days to upset my sister. But, nope, I couldn't think of anything. Everything had been completely normal on the morning of the first day, and as we'd walked to school, and then again at the "doorz."

It was after all the hugging when she'd left us by the doors that everything had changed. I wonder if it had anything to do with school? I mean, she couldn't be mad at me—I hadn't done anything wrong!

I logged onto my computer and as soon as I did, three separate IM boxes popped up. Harlie, Izzy, and Justine, and they all wanted to know what Juliette thought of the picture. I arranged it so we could all chat online in the same IM box.

gOalgirl: sorry, girls. Juliette thought I made the pix of THM on my computer

IzzyBELLA: WHAT???

harliegirl95: u showed her Isabella's pix of Hmonster???

gOalgirl: yup. she thought I was playing with Print Shop or somethin!!!

justME713: No way!

gOalgirl: Swear! I told her Isabella found it on Google and she didn't care!

IzzyBELLA: OMG, that is so WEIRD! Duznt sound like Juliette . . .

harliegirl95: anyway, what happened after lunch, Miss O? How was HMonster?

gOalgirl: > (the wurst!!! Didn't yell at me, but sent a kid to Prin. Sack!!!

harliegirl95: hey, guys, do u think she really wz in JAIL?

justME713: think it wz bc of the chalk?

I had to sign off then, because although I could talk for hours about whether or not the Hinter Monster was ever in jail, and whether or not she ever threw chalk, I had way too much homework to do. And I still wanted to try to Google Hintermeister myself later on. I was hoping Juliette would help me with that, but after our conversation from a few minutes ago, I was figuring that wasn't going to happen.

I finished my math homework and my vocabulary homework, and I was working on my map skills sheet when my mother called me down for dinner. Sheesh! My homework had taken all afternoon to do! If this was the way it was going to be in the Hinter Monster's class, I guess I could count on not having a life for the next ten months.

Downstairs I helped set the table, then I sat in my usual seat at the dinner table across from Juliette. As soon as I did, I noticed she was wearing earphones. She had on her iPod at the dinner table!

My dad noticed, too.

"Juliette, I don't like you to wear that at the dinner table," he said. "You know that."

Juliette sighed. "Come on, Dad! Please? I love this song! Can't I just listen for a little while? Then I'll turn it off. Promise!"

I stared at Dad to see his reaction. No way would he let Juliette wear her earphones at the table! Especially since last month he'd flipped out when I brought the cordless phone into the dining room to finish my conversation with Harlie.

"Well, okay," Dad said finally. "But just for a few minutes more."

My mouth fell open. "But Dad–" I started to say, just as I caught Juliette's glare.

"What, Miss O?" he asked.

I decided not to say anything to give Juliette more reasons to shoot me nasty looks, so I just changed the subject.

"Um, what I was going to say was, Dad, do you and Mom think you can find out about switching me into another class?"

Dad looked at me in surprise. "You don't like the class you're in?" he asked.

Mom sat down and joined in on the conversation. "This is the first I'm hearing of this," she said. "What's the problem, sweetheart?"

The problem? I thought. *Where do I begin?*

"Well," I started, "first of all, my teacher, Mrs. Hintermeister, gives a ton of homework! Even on the first day of school!"

My sister decided she would join in on the conversation and pulled off her earphones. "In middle division, you get twice the normal amount of homework, so I wouldn't complain if I were you! You have it easy!"

I stared at her in disbelief. "Easy?" I cried. "Are you joking? You know what the Hinter Mon . . . uh, Mrs. Hintermeister is like! She's the strictest, hardest teacher in the whole school! Like for tonight, I had three math sheets and—"

My father interrupted me. "Miss O, you've always been a strong student," he said gently. "I'm sure you'll be able to keep up with the work. Your teacher, Mrs. Hinteise . . . Himertis . . . what was it?"

"Hintermeister."

"Well, she probably just needs to get to know the students at this point."

"Sure," my mother chimed in, "she'll soon see what a good student and a hard worker you are, then she'll probably ease up on the assignments."

"But why can't I switch classes? I can't stand this class, really! I mean it! It's the worst! Can't I switch into Isabella's class?"

"They'll never let you switch," Juliette said.

Thanks, big sister! You're a real help!

"Mom? Can't you call to find out?" I pleaded.

My mother shook her head. "I'm sorry, sugar, but Juliette is right. They have a strict 'no switching' policy at Sage. And anyway, you and Harlie were together last year. You should learn now that you won't always be in class with your best friends."

Du-uh! Didn't I know that?

My parents didn't get it. It wasn't even a matter of being in a class with a best friend. I just didn't want to be in *this* class.

My father touched my hand gently. "Listen, honey. Let's give it a few weeks and see how it goes, okay? If you're miserable, we'll re-open the case and have another discussion."

I frowned and cut into my lamb chop. "Re-open the case." That's how dads talk when they are lawyers. Boy, I was so mad! I was really hoping my parents would see how much I wanted out of that class. I wonder if they would change their minds if they knew Hintermeister was a criminal!

I shot a look at Juliette, who had put her earphones back on and had opted out of the family conversation. *Some big help you were!* I said to her but only in my head, not out loud. Whatever happened to sisters sticking together?

"Is there any *good* news to report about school?" my mother asked.

Again, Juliette pulled off her earphones. "Well, in middle division, we have dance education in gym!" she said excitedly. "It's so cool, you can choose to do hip-hop, or jazz, or ballet."

"That sounds great, Juliette," my mom said.

"And in middle division you get to take a foreign language," she went on. "I picked Japanese, isn't that so awesome?"

My father nodded. "Wow, I didn't know they taught Japanese in school. Very awesome," he said with a smile.

"Oh! And the best thing about middle division," Juliette said, "is that they have a whole bunch of writing classes to choose from. I can choose creative writing, or playwriting, or journalism. The teachers are so great, too. They are all so nice!"

Juliette looked at me when she said that, and I have to say, it made me feel even worse than I was already feeling. It was almost like she was bragging about her teachers being so nice, when she knew how awful my teacher was! I was beginning to dislike "middle division Juliette."

"How about with you, Miss O?" Dad asked me. "Anything interesting going on with you?"

I suddenly remembered the baking contest. My eyes lit up and I nodded enthusiastically. "Yes! I almost forgot to tell you!" I said. "They're having a baking contest at school. And the winner gets their recipe entered in a New York State contest, and then the winner of *that* competes nationally!"

My father grinned. "Now *there's* something exciting!" he said. "And I'm guessing you're going to enter, right?"

"You bet!" I said. "Can you help me with the recipe, Mom?" I asked. I didn't really need her help—other than having her supervise my oven use—but I liked doing projects with my mom. Especially baking, because she was so good at it. Much better than my father, who can't cook or bake at all, and who always jokes that he once burned salad.

"Absolutely, honey," Mom said with a smile. "We'll sit down together one night soon and make a few practice runs with whatever recipe you choose to enter. Sound like a plan?"

I nodded happily. Somehow, though I still had a ton of homework waiting for me upstairs, and though my sister was acting like an alien, and though I still had to face my super-awful teacher again in the morning, I was feeling pretty good. With this baking contest, I had something really fun and exciting to look forward to!

Chapter 6
What's Cookin'?

"Okay," I said to my BFFs as we sat outside on the soccer field during recess. "First things first. The Hinter Monster. Anybody have any new information?"

"Not me," Isabella said apologetically. "I didn't go online last night."

Harlie shook her head, too. "Sorry, Miss O. Me neither."

"How about you, Miss O? Weren't you going to ask Juliette to investigate with you?" Justine asked me.

"Well, that *was* my plan," I told them, "but I don't know, Juliette was acting so weird yesterday!" I told them more about how she didn't care about Isabella's picture, and how she totally abandoned me during dinner, when I'd needed her support about switching classes.

"I don't know what's going on with her," I added, "but she's being so secretive and snippy. And last night at dinner? All she did was talk about middle division. It was middle division *this* and middle division *that*."

"Maybe she's just too cool to hang out with now that she's in middle division," Isabella commented.

I hated to admit it, but I was thinking the same thing. Though I couldn't bring myself to say it out loud—after all, Juliette was my *sister*! We usually got along great and I had never trash-talked her to anyone. I didn't want to start now.

"Okay, I'm going to change the subject!" I announced. I opened my messenger bag and pulled out three index cards. "On each card," I told the girls in the most serious voice I could muster, "is one of my favorite recipes. I picked three that I think would be great for the contest, and now, you guys have to vote on one."

I laid out the three cards on the ground, face down. "Whatever recipe you all choose," I said, lowering my voice to add to the drama, "is the one I'm going to enter."

It was quiet for a few seconds, and my friends exchanged looks. Then Justine batted her eyes playfully. "Wow, Miss O!" she gushed. "I just feel so . . . so *honored*!"

Harlie clutched her heart dramatically and gasped. "You mean, you're letting *us* pick the recipe?" she asked in mock surprise.

"Oh, my!" Isabella exclaimed in a completely ridiculous voice. "I think that's just too much responsibility!" Then she pretended to faint.

I made a face at my goofball friends. "Ha-ha," I said dryly. "Come on, guys! This is a big deal to me!"

Isabella punched me playfully. "We're just kidding, you *loser*! Of course, we know it's a big deal! You were just acting so serious, it was funny. Sorry, but we're just joking around with you!"

I let out a grin. "I know, but come on. We only have a little time left for recess. You know how nuts I am about getting back to class before the bell."

The girls all nodded.

"So can I tell you the three recipes?"

Harlie got into her most serious sitting position. "Yes! We're ready now. Shoot!"

Isabella and Justine nodded, too. "Let's hear them," Isabella said.

I cleared my throat. "Okay. The first recipe is something I made for Harlie's birthday last year."

Harlie's eye lit up. "Ooooh, goody!" she squealed.

"Brownie Volcanoes," I said.

Justine licked her lips. "I remember those," she said. "Oh my God, they were *so* good!"

Isabella agreed. "They were awesome, Miss O. With that warm lava fudge inside that oozed out when you bit into them? Yeah, they were amazing. Make those!"

"Yeah, make those!" Harlie agreed.

I laughed. "Well, wait! I have two more," I reminded them.

"Let's hear them," Justine said.

"Okay. The second recipe is for something my dad and I made last Christmas for everybody. Peppermint Bark."

Harlie fell backwards onto the grass. "Oh, man! That was so delish! Wait! Make that, Miss O! Definitely make Peppermint Bark!"

"Which was the Peppermint Bark?" Isabella asked. "That white chocolate stuff you put in tins for everyone?"

"Yes."

Isabella made a face. "No offense, chica, but I didn't really like that. I don't exactly love peppermint."

"I disagree," Justine said diplomatically. "I think it's one of Miss O's best recipes. People who like peppermint will love it. I remember my father liked it so much, he told me he thought Miss O should go into business making the stuff!"

I smiled. "Did he really say that, Justine?" I asked.

Justine smiled back. "Yup. And he ate most of what you gave us, by the way."

Okay, two good recipes so far—except for the Isabella hating peppermint thing, I was on a roll.

"What's the third recipe?" Isabella asked.

I grinned as I read the third index card out loud. "Oatmeal cookies," I said.

"*Ohhhhhhhhh!*" all three of my friends squealed at the same time. Isabella pulled the card from my hands and she actually kissed it. "That's the winner, Miss O! Oatmeal cookies! Definitely! Yours are the best ever!"

"She's right," Justine said. "Forget what I said about the other two recipes. I mean, they're great, but your oatmeal cookies are incredible."

I turned my attention over to Harlie, who was still lying on her back on the grass from the Peppermint Bark episode. She didn't get up, instead she thrust her arm into the air and gave me the surfers "hang-ten" sign. "Oatmeal cookies!" she shouted.

I smiled to myself. I'd had a feeling the oatmeal cookies would win. That's why I'd saved that recipe for last. It was really one of Grandma Mimi's recipes. The cookies always came out so moist and yummy. And they crisped around the edges, too, giving them a real home-baked taste. I'd made them last year for the big soccer club fundraiser and everybody had asked me for the recipe. (No, I didn't give it out—it's mine and Mimi's best-kept secret!)

"So it's settled!" I announced. "Oatmeal cookies it is. Thanks, guys!"

Harlie sat up as we gathered our things to head back to the building. "Do you need any help with the cookies, Miss O?" she asked, licking her lips a little.

Sure!" I told her. "You can come over and help me make a test batch. I'll probably have to make a few of them before I make the batch for next Friday," I explained.

"Great!" Justine said. "We can come over whenever."

"*Hmmmm,*" I muttered out loud. "The only problem is *when?* I mean, I get so much homework every day, and today I have soccer practice after school."

"Maybe over the weekend?" Isabella suggested.

"I guess so," I said. "I have a soccer game on Sunday, so maybe after the game."

"Just tell us when you want us," Justine said, "and we'll be there with spoons and mixing bowls!"

"And baking powder and eggs!" Harlie chimed in.

"And . . . and . . . " Isabella made a face. "You know I know nothing about baking. What do you put in oatmeal cookies anyway?" she asked.

Harlie, Justine, and I exchanged looks, then we burst into laughter.

"Oats!" we shouted at her.

Isabella's face turned red. "Oh, right," she said in embarrassment. "Oats. Makes sense!"

Walking back to class a few minutes later, I thought about how lucky I was to have such great friends. No matter what, they were always there for me.

I guess that's another reason I was feeling so badly about the Juliette-weirdness thing. I mean, here I was about to enter one of my recipes into a really important contest, maybe win a chance to compete nationally, and all my friends were psyched for me except for my BFF.

My own sister.

Chapter 7
Up to My Ears

"What are Oatmeal Drops?" Lindsey whispered to me as she walked past my chair to hand out science vocabulary sheets to everyone in our row.

I looked down at my science notebook and realized I'd been doodling all over my notes about magnets. Well, I wouldn't exactly call it doodling—it was more like I was trying out different names for my oatmeal cookies.

Oatmeal Drops

Oat Boats

Oatmeal Delights

But nothing was quite right. I needed a really catchy, cool name for my cookies—especially if they were going to be sold around the world. I would have to ask the girls to help me choose a name for my cookies. I bet Justine would have some ideas, she was the most creative.

"It's nothing!" I whispered back to Lindsey.

Now normally, I would have told Lindsey about my oatmeal cookies and about entering the contest. After all, she was one of my soccer team-mates on the Wildcats, and we'd been sort of friends for a while, over to each others' houses and stuff, that sort of thing. But after she'd ratted me out for the knee-shaking thing the other day, well, let's put it this way, Lindsey Page was not on my list of favorite people at the moment!

Lindsey made a face at me and kept on walking down the aisle, handing out worksheets. I looked up at the clock for the bazillionth time that afternoon, praying it would just be 3:00 already.

At school, Fridays were the best . . . and worst . . . days of the week, in my opinion. The best because you knew it was the last day of the week and the weekend was almost there. And the worst, because if you're in a class like the Hinter Monster's, the clock always seemed to move super-slow on Fridays!

There were still fifteen minutes left before the end of the day. I glanced over the vocab worksheet on my desk and was relieved to see it was easy. Suddenly, I had a great idea: If I finished it as fast as I could, then turned it in first, I could then ask the Hinter Monster if she would let me hand out the Friday fliers. Maybe do something to get on the teacher's good side for a change. Lindsey was always the one volunteering for everything in class, and Mrs. Hintermeister never seemed to yell at her.

I flew through my vocabulary worksheet in record time (luckily, it was a cinch!), and I popped up from my seat.

"Done!" I said quietly, to myself, really. But Lindsey heard and looked up from her worksheet. I could feel her watching me as I headed toward Mrs. Hintermeister's desk. I couldn't resist flashing her a smile as I walked past.

Sorry, girlfriend! There's a new teacher's pet in town, and her name is Miss O!

Mrs. Hintermeister was writing on the blackboard when I approached her desk to hand in my paper. "Finished, Olivia?" she asked as she wrote.

I smiled sweetly and nodded. "Yup!" I said. "And it's all correct. I know this stuff."

She put down her chalk, picked up my worksheet and began to read. Finally, she placed it back on her desk. "Yes," she said, returning to her writing. "Nice job."

Woo-hoo! I thought. *Now, to continue with my plan . . . .*

"Um, Mrs. Hintermeister?" I said, still standing beside her desk. "Can I pass out the Friday fliers?"

"Do you mean, '*May* I pass out the Friday fliers?'" Mrs. Hintermeister asked without turning around.

Oops! I thought.

"Yes," I replied. "*May* I pass out the Friday fliers?"

"Yes you *may*," she said.

Excellent! I thought as I strolled to the opposite side of the classroom to get the fliers. Every Friday, the Sage School delivers fliers to each classroom for the students to bring home to their parents. Mostly, the fliers were news about PTA meetings and fundraisers. That sort of thing.

As I prepared the fliers for passing out, Mrs. Hintermeister spoke from the front of the room.

"On the blackboard you will find your first book report assignment," she said.

A few kids, including me, groaned. Mrs. Hintermeister ignored us.

"Your book reports will be due next Friday," she went on, "but I strongly suggest you begin reading your book over the weekend. And don't forget to study for the math test on Monday."

Again, we all groaned. Was she kidding? A math test to study for and homework over the weekend? That was so unfair! Every teacher knew that the worst thing they could do to a kid was give homework over the weekend.

Isn't that just great, I thought as I started passing out the bright blue Friday fliers. *More stuff to add to my weekend things-to-do list!*

When I got to Lindsey's desk, I could tell she was mad at me.

"I was going to hand the fliers out today!" she whispered sharply to me. "I can't believe you, Olivia!"

I made a face. "What do you mean you were going to?" I whispered back. "It's not your job—it's anybody's job!"

"But you heard me say to Samantha that I was going to ask to hand them out and that's why you asked—"

Suddenly, Mrs. Hintermeister's voice echoed through the classroom.

"Olivia! Passing out the Friday fliers is not an opportunity to chat with your friends!" she scolded.

Lindsey spun around in her seat and returned to her writing as if she hadn't just been the one chatting. Me? I was left standing there, looking guilty. *Here comes trouble,* I thought. *Trouble with a capital "O."*

"I wasn't chatting," I began.

Mrs. Hintermeister didn't let me finish. "You *weren't?*" she asked. "I'm pretty sure I heard your voice, Olivia."

I groaned. "Well, yes, I was talking, but I didn't start the conversation."

"Either way," Mrs. Hintermeister said matter-of-factly, "that is your third strike for this week, Olivia. Please complete one of the consequences assignments over the weekend."

I stood there, dumbfounded. "Over the weekend?" I asked in disbelief.

"Yes."

"But . . . but . . . that's not fair!" I insisted.

Mrs. Hintermeister's eyes narrowed. "You know my rules," she said. "On the first day of school we went over the code of conduct in the classroom."

"I know, but it wasn't just me!"

"So would you like me to extend the assignment to the entire class?" the Hinter Monster asked.

At once, everyone's eyes were on me. Staring at me, pleading with me not to let the Hinter Monster punish them, too. *Oh, great,* I thought. *A chance for the whole class to hate me? No way!*

It was useless to keep arguing with the Hinter Monster. With every word I said, I was getting deeper and deeper into trouble. The last thing I wanted was to be responsible for the whole class having to do homework over the weekend.

"No," I replied quietly.

"Fine," the Hinter Monster replied.

I finished handing out the dumb fliers, then returned to my dumb desk to wait for the dumb bell to ring.

Fridays, like I said, can be the best and the worst days of the week.

This Friday?

Definitely the worst.

Later that day, Dad picked me up from soccer practice. He was on his cell phone when I got into the car. It sounded as if he were talking to Grandma Mimi.

"Hi, Mimi!" I yelled into the phone.

Juliette and I have called our grandmother "Mimi," ever since I could remember. Dad says it's because when Juliette was a baby, she couldn't say "Grandma" or "Nanny." It just always came out as "Mimi." Like Dad calling me "Miss O"—it just stuck.

"Mimi says 'Hi,' back," Dad told me. A few seconds later, he snapped his phone off. "I just wanted to make sure we were on for tomorrow."

"Tomorrow?" I asked. "What's tomorrow?"

"We're going to Mimi and Poppy's for the day," Dad said. "It's Poppy's birthday tomorrow, so we have a whole thing planned."

Mimi and Poppy live about an hour away from us, and normally I love going to visit them. (For grandparents, they are very cool.) But I was kind of worried about all that I had to do this weekend. There was the consequences assignment and the book report. That was going to take forever. And I'd really wanted the girls to come over to help with my oatmeal cookies this weekend. I had a nagging feeling there was something else for school—but I just couldn't remember what.

Oh, and my first soccer game of the season was this Sunday.

And now Poppy's birthday.

"Are you going to make Poppy a birthday cake?" Dad asked.

I slumped a little in my seat. Poppy's cake. Well, now I had that to do, too. Not that I minded—I love making cakes for Poppy. I make him his favorite cake every year for his birthday: a sugar-free pudding cake. I don't put sugar in it because Poppy is diabetic and can't have sugar. Anyway, even though I was up to my ears in things to do this weekend, how could I not make Poppy his cake?

"Sure," I said, mentally adding that to my weekend list that seemed to be growing by the minute.

"And I guess I'll make him a card, too, like last year," I added.

"He'll love that," Dad said. "Maybe get Juliette to help?"

I stared out the window as we drove. *Yeah, right. My sister who doesn't seem to be talking to me at the moment? A lot of help she'll be.*

After dinner that night, I was in the kitchen, pulling out the ingredients I needed to make Poppy's cake. What I *really* wanted to be doing was test-baking a batch of oatmeal cookies, but I couldn't disappoint my Poppy. Juliette came into the kitchen for a snack, holding the phone to her ear and chatting away. She didn't see me at first, as she reached into the pantry for a pack of microwave popcorn.

She laughed. "That is *so* rich!" she said into the phone. "Totally rockin'! Fabioso! I am all over that! Do you think he will?"

I stared at her, wondering who in the world she would say "fabioso" to.

That's when she noticed me. "Oh! Lemme go," she told her friend. "I can't talk right now."

"Hey," she said to me as she turned off the cordless phone.

"Hey, Juliette. Who was that?" I asked, a little surprised that she had spoken to me.

"No one," she replied. "Nobody you know."

"Oh," I said, feeling hurt. *Why wasn't she telling me stuff anymore?*"

"I'm making popcorn." Juliette said. "Want some?"

"No thanks," I said. I turned the oven to preheat then started mixing some of the cake ingredients together while Juliette's popcorn popped in the microwave.

"Wanna help make Poppy's cake?" I asked. I thought maybe we could work on making the cake together and we'd have so much fun maybe she'd start telling me private stuff again.

"Can't," she said, "I have a book report to do."

"Hey, me too!" I said, sad that she turned me down, but a little excited that we at least had something to be miserable about together: homework on the weekend. "Mine is due on Friday," I added, "but the Hinter Monster said we should read our books over the weekend."

"Mine is due on Wednesday," she said. "We don't get a lot of time to do stuff in middle division. Certainly not a whole week. Middle division is really hard. I can't explain it, but when you're in middle division you'll see what I mean."

I made a face.

"Well fifth grade is hard, too!" I told her. "Especially when you have the strictest teacher in the school! Like today, I was handing out—"

At that moment, the microwave beeped, signaling that the popcorn was ready.

"Can you hand me a bowl?" Juliette asked, totally interrupting me.

I pulled a bowl from the cabinet and handed it to her. So she obviously didn't want to hear about my problems with school.

"Well, can you at least help me decorate Poppy's cake when it's finished?" I asked. "Remember we did that last year and it came out so awesome!"

Well, let me tell you, it was as if I had asked her to do my chores for the next five years—the reaction I got from my sister was, um, crazy!

"You just don't get it, do you?" she said, pouring the hot popcorn into the bowl. She didn't look at me, but I could see her face was all scrunched up and she slowly began freaking out. "I can't help with Poppy's cake! I can't do anything because I have so much work! I'm in middle division now, Miss O! Do you know what that means?"

I was too stunned to answer her.

"It means I'm very, very busy! Middle division is much more important than lower division, Miss O. There's way more work, and your grades really count!"

I watched her pick up the popcorn bowl and storm out of the kitchen.

Okay, I thought, who was that crazy freaking out girl… and what has she done with my sister?

Later that night, I was lying in bed, reading *The Phantom Tollbooth*, the book I had picked for my book report, when Juliette came into my room.

"Can I ask you something?" she said.

"Well that depends," I replied. "Can you actually have a conversation with someone who isn't in middle division?"

Juliette made a face. "Ha-ha," she said. "Sorry for all the drama before," she added. "I'm over it now."

I sat up. "Well good!" I said. "Because you were starting to freak me out a little!"

"Yeah, well . . . I have a lot going on," she said.

See? I'm telling you that this was the most confusing part of it all. Did Juliette think she was the only one in the world with a lot going on?

"I have a lot going on, too," I said.

Juliette sighed. "I know, I know," she said. "I'm sorry I didn't help you make Poppy's birthday cake. I'll make the card, okay?"

"Okay, but it's not only about that—" I began.

Juliette cut me off. "So can I ask you something?" she asked again. "I really need reinforcements. Do you have any?"

"Reinforcements?" I said. "Really?"

Juliette nodded.

"Well, guess what? I *do* have them! I don't know what they are, but Dad bought me two boxes."

"Oh, great!" Juliette said. "I finished handwriting the first part of my book report and then I accidentally ripped the holes in the loose leaf paper. In middle division we have to handwrite our book reports to practice our cursive. Then we're allowed to do it on the computer."

I rolled my eyes to myself as I searched for the reinforcements. To tell you the truth, I was really getting sick of hearing about middle division.

I tossed Juliette the box of reinforcements I kept in my desk drawer and watched how she stuck the little white circles over the torn holes in the loose leaf paper.

"So that's what they're for," I muttered.

Juliette finished fixing all the holes, then handed me back the box. "Thanks," she said, turning to leave my room.

"Wait!" I called out to her. I had just come through for her. Maybe now she might actually come through for me? Prove to me that she was still the same Juliette?

"What?" she asked from my doorway.

"Well, I know you're busy and all—"

"Very busy," she said.

"Right. Very busy," I corrected myself. "But could you please, please,

please help me this weekend? I want to go on the Internet and try to find some more information about my teacher being in jail."

Juliette frowned. "Ugh, Miss O. That's going to take so much time! That picture is probably just a joke somebody posted somewhere. And you and the girls fell for it."

"I don't think it's a joke," I said. "And anyway, I just really want to look online for some more stuff about her. I'm so bad at surfing the Web—I never know what I'm doing. Please?"

"Okay, okay," Juliette finally agreed. Then she left my room.

"Thanks!" I called out after her. Okay, so maybe she was coming back to her old self. Maybe tomorrow morning we could sit together and surf the Web looking for some dirt on the Hinter Monster, and we could laugh and hang out like we used to. Everything would return to normal.

I crossed my fingers and hoped it would happen. Then I fell back on my pillow and got back to my book. Which, I should tell you, was really very funny.

Chapter 8
Like Totally Spun, Dude!

On Saturday morning, I woke up and found I was still in my clothes from the night before. I guess I'd fallen asleep reading, because my book was closed and on my nightstand with a bookmark holding my page, and my lamp was turned off. Mom or Dad must have found me asleep and done all that.

Anyway, there was still an hour before we had to leave for Mimi's and Poppy's, and I was dying to do some undercover investigative work online with Juliette before it was time to go.

Next door, I could hear that Juliette was up, and already on her computer.

"Hey!" I said with a knock on her door. "Can you help me now?" I asked as I stepped inside the room.

Juliette held up a finger to say that I should hold on a second, while she typed an IM with her other hand. I stood there and waited.

"*Woo-Hoo!*" her buddy's sound called out from the computer.

Juliette read her message and laughed. Then she started typing back a message.

"Juliette!" I said impatiently, "I thought we could—"

"Hang on, Miss O!" she replied. "I'm in the middle of something."

I sighed and stood in the doorway, listening to another ten "Woo-Hoo!"s before I just gave up and left.

Back in my room, I got dressed for the trip to Mimi's and Poppy's, then brushed my teeth, pulled my hair into two pigtails, washed up, and checked Juliette's room again.

She was still typing and laughing, so I headed downstairs.

It didn't look like my plan for sisters bonding while surfing the 'Net was going to happen after all.

Later that day, I was playing an intense game of chess with Poppy. I was winning, which was making him crazy because he was the one who'd taught me how to play!

Juliette sat nearby on the sofa, listening to her iPod and watching TV. She had barely said a word to anyone all day! I really don't understand what was up with her. Usually, she's so much fun! Anyway, I was contemplating my next move, when Dad walked into the den and handed Juliette his cell phone.

"It's for you," he said.

My eyes widened. Juliette had given Dad's cell phone number out to her friends? What was she, nuts?

"Make it quick," he added.

Juliette's face brightened as she pulled off her earphones and took the phone from Dad. I was waiting for Dad to say something about not giving out his cell phone number or having her friends call his phone, but he didn't say anything—he just walked out of the room. My jaw was hanging open in shock as Juliette began to chat away.

Poppy glanced at the timer we keep by the chess board to time each other's moves. "Livvy," he said (Poppy is the only one in the world who calls me that. I don't mind, either . . . I kind of like it.) "You have less than a minute," he pointed out.

"Okay," I said. But I could barely concentrate on the game as I tried to catch Juliette's conversation. Who was she talking to? I decided to ask.

"Who is that, Juliette?" I asked.

Juliette covered the mouthpiece. "Just a friend," she said. "Nobody you know."

"Dad lets you use his cell?" I asked, bewildered.

Juliette rolled her eyes. "Talking here!" she said to me. (Obnoxiosity!) Then she continued her conversation. "Supreme, dude! That is *so* spun!"

Poppy and I exchanged looks.

"Spun?" he whispered.

I shrugged. "Don't ask me," I whispered back. I took my chess move, sliding my rook across the board and putting his bishop in jeopardy. "She's been talking all weird like that since she started middle division."

Juliette threw her head back and giggled. "You are too funny," she said as she flipped her hair.

My eyes narrowed at my sister. "Juliette," I said in a loud enough whisper for her to hear, "are you talking to a *boy*?"

She covered the mouthpiece again. "Really, Miss O! Can I have just one conversation in peace?"

I made a face at her. "Sor-ry!" I said. "Sheesh!" I added as Poppy took his next move.

When Juliette was finished with her conversation, she switched off the phone and came over to our table. "For your information, that wasn't a boy, Miss O," she said. "It was Skyler."

"Whatever," I said, pretending I was more interested in the chessboard than in her dumb cell phone conversation.

I have to tell you, it was right then and there that I was starting to feel really hurt by it all. Up until now, Juliette was just being weird and different. I could handle that—whatever. I had assumed it was only because of back-to-school nerves.

But there was something more to Juliette lately. She'd become so distant and obnoxious! I was beginning to feel as if I was losing my best friend.

"I gave her Dad's cell phone number in case she needed to talk to me about the book report," Juliette went on. "I'm like the only girl in middle division without a cell!"

I glanced up at my sister and could tell that this was something that was really bothering her.

"I asked Mom and Dad for a cell for my birthday," she said, "but they said they had to think about it. I really hope they say yes!"

Wow . . . this was *big*! I hadn't known Juliette asked for a cell. How could she not have told me that?

"They said they were thinking about it," I offered, "so that's a good sign."

But Juliette's face had a sour expression. "I know, but I really, really want one. You don't know what it's like to be the *only* girl in school without a cell!"

"Well I don't have one," I pointed out.

Juliette looked at me as if I were from another planet. "Hel-lo?" she said sarcastically, "you're like in *fifth* grade! You can't have a cell phone!"

"Why not?" I asked. "Some kids in my grade have cells," I insisted, knowing full well that Mom and Dad would never get me a cell phone at my age.

Juliette put her hands on her hips. "Oh, never mind!" she said. "You just don't get it!" She spun away and left the room.

I leaned back in my chair and shook my head. "Don't you think she's being all weird?" I asked Poppy.

Poppy thought for a minute. "Well, I wouldn't say she was being weird," he told me. "But something is different about your sister," he agreed. "I wouldn't worry about it," he added. "She's probably just trying to adjust to a new school."

"Well, she'd better hurry it up!" I said, hitting the timer to time Poppy's next move. "Because I'm starting to wish the 'O' in 'Miss O' stood for 'only child!'"

Chapter 9
Goal!

"Go! Go! Go, Miss O!" I heard my dad calling out from the sidelines.

I had the ball and I was dribbling it up the side of the field, looking for an opening where I could cut into the middle and shoot. The team we were playing against was also made up of fifth graders, but they seemed so much *bigger!*

Shifting my eyes from the ball to the goal and back again, I raced past two of my opponents and headed into their defensive zone. Just then, I spotted an opening! I didn't stop to think, I just hooked a turn to the left and set up my shot. It was going to be a left-foot shot, which was my worst. But I had to try. I pulled my foot back—then let loose on the ball.

"Goal!" I heard Coach Schneider cheer from the sideline. The ref blew the whistle, and the Wildcats went crazy, jumping up and down and high-fiving one another. Even Lindsey called out to me, "Way to go, Miss O!"

I had tied the score. I was so happy! So were my parents, who were high-fiving each other, too. And so were Isabella, Harlie, and Justine, who had come to watch my game.

With a huge smile across my face, I looked around for Juliette, who always gives me the thumbs-up after a good play, but I couldn't find her in the crowd. Strange, I thought. Juliette's never missed any of my soccer games. Just like I've never missed any of her tennis matches.

The game ended a few minutes later in a tie, and after a quick meeting with Coach Schneider, I headed toward my parents, who were waiting to congratulate me and take me and the girls home.

"Great game!" Dad said with a smile. He gave me a big bear hug.

"Awesome goal!" Mom added, kissing me on the cheek. (I didn't mind, if that's what you were thinking. I'm actually very mushy when it comes to my parents. Even in public!)

"Where's Juliette?" I asked them.

"She's at home," Dad said. "Finishing her book report."

"She's home all by herself?" I asked.

Dad smiled. "Well, sweetie, we're only a few blocks away, and I have my cell in case she needs me. She's ready for some more responsibility, you know. She's in middle division now."

I rolled my eyes. *Of course I knew she was in middle division! How could I not? Juliette only reminded me of it a trillion times a day!*

"I guess," I said with a shrug. "But she never misses my games," I added.

"Don't worry!" Mom promised, "We'll be sure to tell her about every play! We'll even act it out for her if you want!"

I smiled, picturing my parents acting out my soccer game. It was funny, and Juliette would laugh her head off, but it really wasn't the same thing.

In the car on the way home, Isabella, Harlie, Justine, and I chatted about the game and then about the test-batch of cookies we were about to bake. When we got home, we found Juliette in the kitchen, working on her book report.

"How was the game?" she asked. I thought her voice sounded a little funny. You know, kind of upset, maybe, that she'd missed it?

"It was great," I told her. "We were losing, three to two, but I scored the tying goal."

Juliette's eyes widened. "Wow, that's great, Miss O!" she said. She sounded like she'd meant it, too.

"Thanks," I said.

"Sorry I missed it," she offered. "But, I have all this work."

I shrugged. "Yeah, I know. Whatever," I said, trying not to sound hurt. "Do you think you'll be finished soon?" I asked. "Because we're going to bake. You know, practice for the contest. Maybe you can help, too?"

"I don't know," Juliette said hesitantly. "I just have so much to do. In sixth grade you have to do weekly book projects, which are a lot like reports but . . . ."

I sighed, then turned toward the girls as she was talking. It was probably very rude of me, but to tell you the truth, I couldn't hear another word about sixth grade, middle division, or any of Juliette's other problems.

Juliette kept on explaining her difficult books reports and "advanced" homework assignments to us as she gathered her things together.

"I'll finish working upstairs," she told us.

"Maybe if you finish soon, you can hang with us?" Harlie asked.

"Maybe," Juliette replied. "But I'll probably be working all day. And all night!"

"Bummer," Isabella said.

When Juliette was gone, we began to pull baking sheets and mixing bowls out from the kitchen cabinets and set up a baking work space.

"So has your sister been that intense about school all week?" Justine asked.

I let out a snort. "You don't know the half of it," I commented.

"Weird," Harlie said. "I mean, we haven't seen your sister all week. You'd think she'd want to hang with us for a while."

I shrugged as I headed for the refrigerator to get the butter, milk, and eggs. "Welcome to my world!" I said. "She hasn't hung out with me all week, either. She just spends day and night talking to her new, secret friends like Skyler. Oh, and did I tell you she wants a cell?"

Isabella's eyes widened. "Really?" she asked. "I would kill for a cell! Is she getting one?"

"Don't know. She asked Mom and Dad and they said they'd think about it." I told them.

"That would be so cool for you guys," Harlie said.

I laughed. "Well, it would be cool for Juliette," I said. "But I doubt she would ever let me use it. She's barely talked to me all week! And she doesn't tell me anything anymore."

Justine put her hand on my shoulder. "That stinks, Miss O."

I nodded. "Yeah. I guess she's just really into her new life in sixth grade."

"Her new life?" Justine asked in confusion.

"Yeah," I replied. "Her new life in middle division. It's always 'middle division this' and 'middle division that,' like it's such a big difference from lower division and that her life has changed so dramatically."

"Has it?" Isabella wanted to know.

I shrugged, placing the eggs on the counter far away from the edge so that they wouldn't roll off. "Who knows?" I said. "I mean, she says she has a ton of work and all, but I have a ton of work, too! Meanwhile, she won't even listen to any of my problems. She's been too wrapped up in her own."

Isabella felt bad for me. "Wow. Sorry, Miss O."

I smiled at my friends. They were really so understanding. "The whole thing stinks," I told them. "I feel like I don't have a sister anymore. But at least I still have you guys!"

Suddenly, Harlie's eyes widened. "Oh! I totally forgot to tell you! Do you know what I heard on Friday on the bus coming home from school?"

We all looked at Harlie. "No, what?" I asked.

Harlie lowered her voice and leaned in toward us. "Well, some of the kids from middle division were talking," she said, "about Mrs. Hintermeister."

My eyes narrowed. "Really?" I asked. "What did they say?"

"Something about her being in jail?" Isabella asked hopefully.

"No. Not about that," Harlie replied. "They were talking about how mean she is."

"No kidding," I muttered.

"And then one of them said that when her older sister had Hintermeister, at the end of the year she left a girl back and didn't move her up to sixth."

"But we've heard that before," Justine pointed out.

"Yeah, we know all that already," Isabella added.

"I know, but she also said that when the girl was left back, she had to repeat fifth grade all over again. In Hintermeister's class!"

I gasped. "Are you kidding?" I asked. That was unbelievable.

"No way!" Isabella insisted. "The Hinter Monster for two years straight?"

It was too horrible for me to even think about. How could anybody survive the dungeon of dread for two years straight?

Harlie nodded. "That's what I heard. Another girl said she'd heard that story, too."

Justine shook her head in disbelief. "That's just terrible," she said.

I sat back in my seat. "Terrible?" I said. "I think it would be worse than terrible! I would beg my parents to switch schools! Or to move!" I told them. "I could never, ever have the Hinter Monster twice!"

"But you won't ever have to, Miss O," Harlie told me. "You're a good student. Probably the smartest kid in your class."

I shrugged. "Maybe," I said. "But just thinking about that story freaks me out, Harlie! Can we all swear not to talk about it anymore?"

Everyone nodded.

"Deal!" Isabella said. "No more talking about you-know-who! We came here to help Miss O with cookies, so let's get cracking! Ooooh, that reminds me! Are there any eggs to crack for the cookies? I love to crack eggs! Can I do that, please?"

I giggled. "Sure," I promised. "You can do all the egg cracking."

"And what can we do?" Harlie asked. "I mean, I'm not the best cook in the world you know. Except maybe for my cold noodles in sesame sauce. I am amazing at making that!"

"But they *are cold* noodles," Isabella pointed out. "There's nothing to cook."

"Yes, there is!" Harlie corrected her. "You have to cook the noodles in water. Then you have to mix ingredients."

"But it's not really cooking," Isabella said.

"Yes it is!" Harlie insisted.

We were never going to get anywhere. "Hey, guys!" I said loudly. "Can we just focus on the cookies?"

The girls nodded.

"Yeah, sorry Miss O," Harlie said.

"Me, too," Isabella added with a smile.

I took a seat on the stool by the counter. "Okay then. There are two things we need to do before we bake," I told them.

"And then we can go jump on the trampoline?" Harlie asked. She loved our trampoline. Actually, we all loved playing on the trampoline, but Harlie loved it the most. She's a great gymnast, so she was the best at it, too.

"Yes!" I told her. I was growing a little impatient. "Then we can hang out on the trampoline!"

"So what are the two things?" Justine asked.

"Okay, the first is coming up with a cool name for the cookies," I said. "And the second is coming up with a special ingredient I can put in the cookies that will make Grandma Mimi's oatmeal cookie recipe more like my own."

Justine made a face. "Oh, is *that* all," she joked.

"Well, we don't have to decide on the ingredient today," I said. "I'd like to try out a few different things. But I would really appreciate your suggestions."

Isabella found a pencil and paper and got started right away. "Okay. Names," she said, tapping her pencil on the counter. "Something oatmeal-ish and cookie-ish."

"Something that sounds tasty," Harlie added.

"And something that sounds great with your name," Justine chimed in.

I thought for a second. "Miss O's . . . "

"Outrageous . . ." Harlie said.

"Over-the-top . . ." Justine added.

"Oh-my-goodness-they're-good . . . " Isabella joined in.

"Official!"

"Original!"

"Okay!"

"Hold on a sec!" I said. "Who said, 'Okay?'"

We all laughed.

"Miss O's Okay Cookies? Not so great!" I said with a laugh.

"My bad!" Harlie piped up. "I said it! I just got carried away with the O words."

"Well, let's stick to the oatmealy words," Isabella suggested.

"Hey! How about Miss O's Oatmealies?" Justine proposed.

"I like that!" I said.

"Or, Miss O's Really Oatmealy Cookies?" Isabella offered.

"Darn! I like them both," I said with a sigh. "How about we think about those two names and decide later on during the week?"

The others nodded in agreement.

I smiled brightly. "Settled then! See, that was quick! Now how about some suggestions for a special ingredient?" I asked them. "Oatmeal cookies always have raisins, but I don't like raisins."

"Yuck, me either," Isabella admitted. "Raisins and peppermint. Blech!"

"So I guess you would really hate—peppermint raisin cookies," Harlie joked.

"Yes! And mushrooms!" Isabella added. "I also hate mushrooms!"

"Gross, Isabella! Mushrooms in cookies?" Justine asked.

"No! Just mushrooms in general. I hate them!" Isabella insisted. "They're so squishy and icky and—"

"Um, hel-lo?" I called out, interrupting them. "Can we get back to the subject here?"

"Right. Sorry. Um, how about chocolate chips?" Isabella suggested.

"Or peanut butter chips?" Harlie said.

"Coconut?" Justine asked.

Just then—and I don't know why it was just then—I thought about Mimi and the crêpes she'd showed me how to make yesterday at her house. Crêpes are like pancakes, but thinner. Mimi said they eat crêpes in France. We made a bunch of apple crêpes for lunch yesterday, and they were delish! Anyway, thinking about the crêpes gave me an idea for the most perfect ingredient I could add to my cookies. Something that was just different enough to make the cookies special, but not something that was way-out-there weird: apples!

"Apples!" I cried.

The girls all stared at me, then Justine grinned. "That sounds great, Miss O," she said.

"Baked apple pieces," I went on. "With cinnamon! Just like the apple crêpes my grandmother made yesterday!"

"Mmmm, I love crêpes," Justine said. "They make them in France, you know."

I took out the leftover crêpes I'd stored in the fridge, heated them in the microwave, and gave everyone a taste.

"Oooh! These are so good!" Harlie gushed.

"Great idea, Miss O!" Isabella agreed. "Putting cinnamon apples in your oatmeal cookies will be a huge hit!"

I grinned, picturing the judges' faces when they bit into my moist, delicious, Miss O's Outrageously Okay Really Oatmeally (or whatever we were going to call them) Cookies!

"Okay, so Harlie, you're in charge of peeling the apples," I instructed. "Justine, you can start the recipe by mixing the butter and sugars together. And Isabella, you are flour and eggs."

"Yipee!" Isabella shouted as she clapped her hands together.

As we mixed and chopped and stirred and measured, I felt so grateful for having the three greatest BFFs in the world. I only wished my sister had been downstairs mixing, chopping, stirring, and measuring with us.

Chapter 10
A D+ Day

Monday morning came, and I have to tell you, I was feeling pretty great. I'd spent the whole weekend away from the dungeon of dread, I'd scored a goal in my first soccer game of the season, and best of all, the test batch of oatmeal cookies had come out great.

I'd decided last night not to think about the Hinter Monster and all the rumors about her. I couldn't let those rumors get to me. Harlie was right— I was a good student! I'd always gotten good grades. Hundreds on all my spelling tests, and As on all my math speed tests!

I would never get left back with those good grades. I would never have to face spending two years with the Hinter Meister. No way!

So I was feeling pretty good this morning. So good, in fact, that I was on my way to class . . . *early*!

Yes, this was the new me. The new Miss O, who was going to absolutely try her best not to give Mrs. Hintermeister any reason whatsoever to pick on her. Who was going to keep her mouth shut tight in class and not let Lindsey bother her. And who was going to stare straight ahead at the blackboard the whole day, and listen to every single word her teacher said.

I was going to be perfect!

Fifth grade was going to be perfect!

Life was, from now on, going to be perfect.

I took my seat, unpacked all the stuff from my messenger bag neatly into my desk, and settled in for the morning. I laid out two perfectly sharpened pencils and pulled my math books out of my desk. I was ready for the first lesson of the day.

With a big smile, I leaned back in my seat and glanced at the clock. Five minutes until the bell . . . and I was all ready!

That's when the blackboard caught my eye.

At first it didn't hit me. But after a few seconds, I began to realize that Mrs. Hintermeister had written out math problems on the blackboard. I froze. At the top of the board it said:

> ### TODAY'S MATH TEST:
> ### YOU HAVE 30 MINUTES TO
> ### ANSWER THESE 15 PROBLEMS.
> ### KEEP YOUR EYES ON
> ### YOUR OWN PAPER!

I really couldn't move for a few seconds—I was too shocked. There was a math test this morning, and I had completely forgotten about it!

I felt panicky as I flipped open my textbook and frantically searched for the pages on fractions. How could I have forgotten about the test? She'd told us last Thursday, and then reminded us again on Friday! I even took home my textbook to study! How could this have happened?

I took a deep breath and started to look over the chapter. I was trembling as I read . . . how was I going to memorize this stuff in two minutes?

When the bell to begin class rang, Mrs. Hintermeister wasted no time.

"Books off your desks," she announced. "You have a half-hour to complete this test. Copy down these problems and begin. Please show all work."

Before I knew it, there was scrap paper on my desk, and the clock was ticking away.

I stared at the board. My mind was one great big blank! With a shaky hand, I started writing. But I couldn't focus. The fractions just sort of sat on my page and looked up at me. They looked foreign to me and I couldn't concentrate.

I was going to fail this test!

Later in the cafeteria, I sat with my head down on the table, listening to my friends, but not really hearing them. All I could hear were the voices of my disappointed parents and what they were going to say when they heard I'd failed a test.

"Olivia," my father would say, "Your mother and I are very disappointed in you."

"A failing grade?" my mother would ask in a shocked voice. "How could you?"

Ugh. I was so miserable, I couldn't even eat my mac and cheese, which is my all-time fave lunch at school.

"Miss O?"

I groaned. "What, Isabella?" I asked.

"We were wondering if you were going to sit up and join the conversation?" she asked.

I groaned again. "No."

"Come on, Miss O!" Harlie insisted. "Stop thinking about the math test. So what if you did badly? You can make it up!"

I sat up and shrugged. "I know," I said. "But I'm just so mad at myself for forgetting!"

"Well you have to lighten up," Justine said. "It's not the end of the world. It's just one bad grade. And," she added, "you don't even know how you did on the test! Wait until you get it back to see your grade! I'll bet you did better than you think!"

I shook my head. "I don't think so," I told her. "I was so freaked out, I forgot how to do the math."

"Okay! I have an idea!" Isabella said suddenly. "Let's talk about the names for the cookies. It will take your mind off the math test. Did you decide which one you liked better?" she asked.

"Actually," I said, sort of happy Isabella had changed the subject, "I thought I'd like a combination of the two. Miss O's Really Oatmealies."

"Hey! Cool!" Harlie said. "I like that!"

"Me, too," Justine added.

"Then it's settled!" Isabella said. "Miss O's Really Oatmealies!"

I smiled at my friends. Okay, it was working. I was feeling a little better talking about the cookies. And Justine was right—failing one test wasn't going to ruin my life. It's not like I was going to get left back or anything . . .

"Oh my gosh!" Isabella said suddenly. "Look! It's Juliette!"

I spun around in my seat to see where she was pointing. I didn't see my sister.

"Huh? Where?" I asked.

"Over there!" Isabella said. "She's sitting with those girls over there!"

What? What girls?

I scanned the cafeteria tables until my eyes rested on my sister. There she was, sitting with a group of girls from her grade—and a few I didn't recognize—eating lunch and pretending we weren't in the same cafeteria!

I couldn't believe it!

"That's so rude!" Justine said. "She must have known we were here! We've sat at this same table every day for two years!"

"She's totally ignoring us!" Isabella added.

"What is her problem?" Harlie demanded.

That's what I was thinking. It was one thing to act all weird to me at home and stuff, but to totally diss me and my friends—who were supposed to be *her* best friends—was so not cool.

"Come on," I said, getting up.

The girls followed me over to Juliette's table.

"Juliette?" I said when I got to her table.

Juliette looked up at us. "Um, it's *Jules*," she said with a strange look on her face.

We all exchanged looks.

"What gives?" I asked her. "You're not Juliette anymore?"

In front of her friends, "Jules" rolled her eyes obnoxiously. "I hate that name," she said. "Everyone calls me Jules now."

My eyes widened. "Oh. Well, sorry, but I didn't get the official memo about your name change," I said in a nasty tone.

My sister made a face at me. "What are you guys doing here?" she asked.

"We were going to ask you the same thing," I said. "What are *you* doing here?"

Juliette brightened a bit. "Oh, we thought we'd come eat lunch over here today," she said. "You know, just for old times' sake!"

Her friends laughed.

"But I thought you hated the *really long walk* to this cafeteria?"

Juliette laughed nervously. "Um, do you guys want to sit with us?" she asked.

"No," I answered quickly. "We have something else to do." We didn't, but I didn't want to sit with Juliette—or Jules, or whoever she was today—and her friends. I was steaming mad at her at the moment! I mean, she'd been in the cafeteria this whole time and she hadn't even come over to our table!

"Okay, well I'll see you later!" Juliette said to us, all friendly-like. As if she hadn't totally and completely insulted her best friends in the world.

We left the cafeteria and headed outside. It was a really windy day to be hanging out outdoors, but having just said we had somewhere else to go, we'd had to go *somewhere*. And this was the only other place we could go, so we had to brave the wind.

"Can you believe her?" Isabella asked with a *humph* when we were outside. She pulled her sweatshirt a little tighter around herself.

"Who?" I asked, my voice dripping with sarcasm. "Jules?"

Harlie rubbed her bare arms to warm them because she hadn't taken her sweatshirt to lunch. "She is just so unfriendly! Acting like Miss Sophistication, now that she's in middle division!"

"Obviously," Justine added, "your sister doesn't want to hang out with us anymore. I guess we're just too immature for her—being a whole year younger and all!"

"Well, I'll tell you one thing," I said, silently wishing lunch period would end so we could go back inside to where it wasn't so cold. "I don't think I want to hang with *her* anymore. And sister or not—I'm not going to!"

Moments later I felt horrible, staring at the big, red D+ on the top of my math test. This was the worst grade I had ever received in my entire life. I couldn't believe it. I mean, I know I didn't study for the test because I forgot about it, but looking at the math problems now, I realized I actually *knew* this stuff! I could have gotten the answers all right, if I hadn't panicked like I did.

D+. It didn't seem real.

"Disappointing," Mrs. Hintermeister told me as I approached her desk.

"I know," I said quietly. "Um, do these grades count?" I asked.

My teacher looked at me. "Of course they count," she said.

My heart sunk. I started to walk away, to return to my seat, when Mrs. Hintermeister made an announcement to the class.

"For those of you who did poorly on the test," she said, "you have a chance to earn back half credit."

My ears perked up.

"Tonight, in addition to your homework, you can rework the problems you got wrong. Hand them in tomorrow morning, and you will receive half-credit for every correct answer."

Wow!, I thought. *That was actually nice of her! She was giving us a chance to raise our grades!*

And that was a chance I was *not* going to pass up. Even though it meant doing more work on top of the homework I already had for that night, I was determined to bring up my math grade. I calculated that if I reworked what I got wrong and got the new answers all correct, the best I could get was a B.

And that would be just fine with me!

The bad news was I would have to tell the girls we couldn't hang out together after school today like we'd planned. They would feel bad, but I'm sure they would understand.

As for my other big problem—you know, "Jules"—I was thinking that tonight I would march into her bedroom and tell her exactly what a you-know-what she's been for the past week.

Chapter 11
Confronting Juliette

I could smell Mom's famous baked ziti from all the way up in my room as I sat at my desk and redid the fraction equations from my math test. My homework was taking forever tonight, and since I'd skipped snack after school, after barely touching my mac and cheese lunch, my stomach was growling like crazy! I couldn't wait to take a bite of Mom's ziti. It was my favorite dish!

Downstairs, I heard the front door open and my sister and Dad come in from Juliette's tennis lesson. Juliette ran up the stairs and burst into my room, all excited about something.

"Guess what?" she asked me, breathlessly.

I turned from my homework to face her, wondering why she was suddenly acting all cheery and friendly.

"What?" I replied.

Juliette was grinning from ear to ear. "I made the finals!" she gushed. "In the tennis tournament! It's just down to me and three other girls!"

Honestly, I was thinking that Juliette's news was incredible, but I totally didn't want her to see that I was happy for her. I mean, after what had happened at lunch, why would I want her to know that I cared?

"That's nice," I said, matter-of-factly. Then I turned back to my homework.

"Miss O!" Juliette said loudly. "Didn't you hear what I said? The finals! I made the finals!"

"I know," I replied. "That's really great, *Jules*."

I knew she could tell from the way I said "Jules" that I was mad at her.

"Miss O? What's the matter?" she asked.

I spun around to face her. "Are you joking?" I asked in disbelief. "You don't know?"

Juliette shook her head. "No. What's going on? I thought you'd be all happy for me and everything. But you're acting like you don't care."

I stared at my sister. "Juliette! You've barely spoken to me all week! And you haven't cared about anything I've had to say, either! You've been so mean and unfriendly to me and to the girls, too, why should I even care about your tennis tournament?" I knew it was a lot to lay on her at once, but as soon as I got started, I couldn't stop myself.

"You haven't helped me online, when I asked you a million times," I went on. "You didn't listen to any of my problems with the Hinter Monster, or even offer to help me with my homework or anything! You didn't come over to us in the cafeteria—even though we're your best friends—and then when we came over to you, you were obnoxious and treated us like jerks! And, not to mention," I added, continuing to count out all the bad things she'd done on my fingers, "you didn't come to my first soccer game!"

I folded my arms across my chest, and could feel my face getting redder and redder. I didn't care. I wanted my sister to know I was mad.

I think she knew. Her expression was pretty intense. I even thought she might start crying.

"I'm, um, sorry," she said quietly.

"Well!" I couldn't think of what to say. I guess I wasn't expecting to hear her to apologize. "Good then!" I managed. "But it's not just me who's noticed how you've been this past week," I told her. "The girls have noticed, too."

Juliette stared at the floor.

"You haven't talked to anybody in a whole week and you didn't hang with us yesterday in the kitchen, either. They all think you hate them."

"That's crazy! I don't hate them!" Juliette said.

"But it seems like you do," I said. "And all you do is talk about middle division, all the time! It's so annoying! It's like now that you're in middle division you don't want anything to do with your friends anymore. You don't need us hanging around anymore!" I was starting to get all choked up. But maybe I had just figured it all out? Maybe that's what the whole thing boiled down to? Juliette didn't need us anymore. She didn't need *me* anymore.

"But that's not how I feel," Juliette said. "I still need you guys. It's just that it's been hard in middle division. It's been hard meeting new people and making new friends. And the work has been . . ." her voice trailed off. "Look. Just forget it, okay?" she said finally. "You wouldn't understand!"

I scoffed. "Are you kidding?" I asked. "Do you think you're the only one who has a lot of work?" I picked up my D+ test and waved it out in front of me. "We *all* have a lot of work!" I said. "But best friends are supposed to be there for each other. To help each other and stuff! You haven't helped one bit! You've just been mean and—"

Juliette's eyes widened. "Is that a D+?" she asked.

Embarrassed, I hid my test paper behind my back.

"Wow, you never got a D before," she commented. "Ever!"

"I know," I said. "But since when do you care? You would have known I was having trouble in school if you had bothered to talk to me once this past week. But you didn't. So why should I care one tiny bit that you made the tennis finals?"

Juliette stood in my doorway, with a strange expression on her face. She seemed about to say something, but then she just turned around and walked away.

When she was gone, I fell on my bed. I felt terrible. My sister and I almost *never* fought. It had been hard to tell her all those things, but I was just so angry!

On my bed, I tried my best to hold back the tears. The last thing I wanted was for Juliette to hear me crying. So instead, I took a few more deep breaths and went downstairs for dinner.

It was dark in my room, as I tossed and turned that night. I glanced over at my alarm clock and saw that it was 11:20 p.m. Yikes! It was so late! But I couldn't sleep because so many things were turning inside my head.

My fight with Juliette, for one thing. But I was also worried about my schoolwork. As I lay there trying to sleep, I couldn't help but think of all the bad things that could happen. Like, what if I forgot about another test and got another D? And what if Mrs. Hintermeister didn't let me make up another grade? Would I get left back? Would I be the girl at the Sage School that everybody talked about a few years from now? The girl who was a good student and all . . . but got left back anyway?

And I thought about my sister. I really missed her, to be honest with you.

I missed having a sister I could hang out with. And I wondered if this was the way it was going to be from now on. That the group would be just me, Isabella, Harlie, and Justine, and no more Juliette?

That would be really weird.

Suddenly, my thoughts were interrupted by a quiet "*Moo!*"

And then another. "*Moo!*"

That was Isabella's IM sound!

I got out of bed and reached for my computer mouse to activate my screen.

> **IzzyBELLA:** Miss O! Are you awake?
> **IzzyBELLA:** Miss O???

I looked at the clock again. It was 11:24 p.m. What was Isabella doing on the computer so late??? As quietly as possible, I typed back.

> **gOalgirl:** what r u doing up?
> **IzzyBELLA:** never mind! im sending you something about THM. check your email!

I checked my email and found something from Isabella. I waited for it to open, and when it did, there was a link. I clicked it and a newspaper article came up:

JASMINE APPLEGATE
TO WED RESTAURATEUR
ALAN HINTERMEISTER

Beneath the headline was a picture of Mrs. Hintermeister—she was even younger than in the first picture. Again, she had a big smile, and this time she was dressed in a long, white wedding gown!

My jaw fell open. I had no idea my teacher was married! But before I could say anything, I heard footsteps down the hall. I snapped off my computer and jumped back into bed.

Chapter 12
D-I-S-A-S-T-R-O-U-S

The following morning, Isabella and I waited by the "doorz" for Justine and Harlie. I had IM'd them earlier in the morning to tell them to meet us before school— it was that important.

It was getting late and Harlie's bus hadn't yet come in. Finally, we saw her running toward us.

"So what's the big news?" Harlie asked, slightly out of breath.

I showed them the picture.

"Wow! Look how young she was!" Justine said.

"Pretty gown," Harlie commented. "What's a 'restaurateur'?"

"Someone who owns restaurants," Isabella said.

"Where did you get this picture, Miss O?" she asked me.

I didn't have too much time to talk, so I filled them in quickly as best I could. "Isabella found it last night," I told them.

"I Googled," she admitted. "But my mother said I could," she added, "just as long as I have something in mind to search for and I'm just not Googling whatever."

"How'd you find it?" Harlie asked.

"Well, I suddenly realized that I had first Googled Mrs. Hintermeister's married name," Isabella explained. "But if I wanted more information, I should search under her maiden name—the name she had before she got married."

"I didn't even know the Hinter Monster was married," Justine commented.

"Me either," Harlie said.

"Neither did I," I said.

"I had heard that she used to be Miss Applegate," Isabella told us. "So I went online late last night and Googled 'Applegate.'"

Just then the warning bell rang.

"Well, you know what you have to do now," Harlie told me. "You have to keep Googling her old last name until you find something about her being in jail."

"Right," I said, nodding. "But tomorrow is the contest and I have to bake tonight. Plus, my book report is due tomorrow, and I'm sure I'll have a ton of homework, too! So it looks like the Googling will have to be done this weekend. Can you guys maybe come over to help?" I asked.

The girls all nodded eagerly.

"You bet!" Isabella said.

"Definitely," Harlie added. "I can't wait to get to the bottom of this!"

"Miss O," Justine asked, "what are you going to do if you find out that Mrs. Hintermeister really spent time in jail?"

I shrugged, not having thought about that yet. "I'm not sure," I told them. "But I suppose I'll have to tell someone. And she'll probably get fired, right?"

The girls nodded, and no one said a word. That would be something, to be responsible for getting your teacher fired, huh?

And that was how I went to class that morning. Feeling a little uneasy that I was about to blow the whistle on my teacher.

Well, you should know that if I was feeling uneasy when I walked into class, it wasn't long before I stopped feeling the least bit guilty! The Hinter Monster was especially horrible all morning, and I was kind of wishing the police would break down the classroom door in the middle of our spelling lesson and take her away!

First of all, even though Cody had brought cupcakes to school for his birthday, Mrs. Hintermeister refused to let him pass them out during class. "You may hand them out at the end of the day for after school," she'd told him.

How crazy is that?

Then, when we were in the middle of our history lesson, she broke us up into groups of three and she put me with the two worst kids in the class: Susan and Josh Belsky. They were twins, who, for some reason, had been put in the same class this year. The three of us were supposed to be working on creating a map and a map key, but Susan spent the half-hour coloring in her notebook, and all Josh did was make rude noises under his armpit.

The worst part happened when Josh got caught messing around with another boy in the class. Then all the boys started goofing around and the Hinter Monster freaked out and started yelling at *all of us*.

"The entire class will remain in the classroom during recess today!" she ordered as punishment. "After you get your lunches, you will all report back to the classroom and sit quietly for the duration of the lunch period!"

Talk about awful! The most un-fun thing in the world was to have to stay in the classroom during recess. I was so mad!

When it was time for lunch, I sat at my desk and ate my sandwich, growing angrier with each bite. My teacher was just *so mean*! How could she punish us all when she knew it was just the dumb boys who'd misbehaved? I was beginning to think it wasn't so surprising that she'd been in jail.

I finished my lunch, and took out my book report on *The Phantom Tollbooth*. If I had to stay inside, I might as well work on my report, I figured. But it was hard to concentrate. I wondered what my friends were thinking, sitting in the cafeteria right at that very moment. Surely they were wondering where I was! They were probably laughing and goofing off, having a grand old time.

I groaned. This was so lame! I should be there laughing and goofing around with them! But no. Instead, I'd been sentenced to spending the whole day locked up in the dungeon of dread! For a crime I didn't even commit!

That night, things got worse.

It was 7:30 p.m. and my mother was still in her office in the basement, working with a client on an emergency project. Normally that wouldn't have been such a disaster, but it was my last night before the contest, and she'd promised to help me bake the cookies.

"Mom?" I called downstairs. "Mom?"

"Olivia, I'm still on the phone! I promise I'll be right up as soon as I'm off!"

Just then, Dad came into the kitchen. "What do you need, sweetie?" he asked.

"Dad, I need your help!" I said. I noticed my voice sounded slightly panicky.

Dad smiled hopelessly. "Come on, Miss O! You know I'm a jinx in the kitchen! I can't make a thing! You and your mother are the cooks in this family. Remember that time I burned the salad?"

It was true: Dad had once burned salad. It was the family joke. He'd been preparing a salad and moved the colander off the counter to make more room to cut vegetables. When he did, he accidentally put it too close to something cooking on the stove and the colander caught fire and burned the salad inside.

But I didn't need his help with cooking at the moment.

"No baking or cooking, Dad. I promise. I need you to set up your laptop computer in the kitchen for me," I told him.

"Sure," he said. "How come?"

"Well, I need to bake these cookies and finish typing up my book report," I said.

"Wow," Dad muttered. "Isn't that a lot to concentrate on at once?" he asked.

I nodded. "Yup. And I also have to finish my homework," I added.

"Are you sure you can manage?" he asked me. "I can help you type, if you'd like, after I finish some work I have from the office."

"Sure," I said. "But I need to get started anyway."

I took out all the ingredients for the oatmeal cookies and the utensils and bowls I'd need for baking. I set everything down on the kitchen island counter. Then I pulled out my book report and laid it out on the other end of the counter. Finding a bit more open space left at the end of the counter, I took out my homework and placed it down there.

What I needed, I decided, was a system. A way I could get everything done at the same time. A little mixing, a little typing, a little math. Then a little more mixing, a little more typing, and a little spelling.

Shouldn't be too difficult, right?

Dad came in and set up his laptop for me.

"Should I turn on the oven?" he asked.

I nodded. "Yes, thanks, Dad. You can preheat it to 350 degrees."

"Oh. Um, this button?" he asked.

I shot him a look. "Really, Dad? You don't know how to preheat the oven?"

Dad put his hands on his hips. "Yes, Olivia," he said, "I know how to preheat the oven! I was just was making sure it was the right button. Last time when I thought I'd turned the oven on, I had only actually turned on the oven *light*. A common mistake."

I sighed. "Yes. That's the button."

"Great! Anything else?" he asked.

"No, Dad. I'm good."

As soon as Dad left the kitchen, I started my system. I unwrapped the butter sticks and opened the brown sugar box, and I put the ingredients into a big mixing bowl. Then I looked for the regular sugar, but it wasn't in its usual place in the pantry.

"Dad?" I called out. "Where's the sugar?"

"I don't know!" Dad called back. "Did you look in the pantry?"

I groaned. Dad wasn't going to be of any help, I decided. Maybe Juliette could help me? I thought.

"Dad?" I called out a third time.

"Yes?"

"Where's Juliette?" I asked.

"She's at tennis!" Dad called back. "I'm picking her up later!"

Well, that was just great. The one night I needed everybody's help—nobody was around! That settles it, I thought. I'm on my own.

I searched for a long time until I finally found the blue plastic sugar container in the pantry, buried behind some boxes of flour in the way, way back. Mom must have moved it to a new place because we usually keep it up front with the brown sugar and powdered sugar. I measured out what I needed and tossed it into the bowl with the brown sugar and the butter. As I mixed, I carried the bowl over to where my spelling words were and began to practice spelling.

"Annoying," I said, quizzing myself out loud. "As in, 'Spelling tests are annoying.' A-N-N-O-Y-I-N-G."

I kept mixing.

"Fabulous," I went on. "As in, 'Wouldn't it be fabulous if I could switch teachers?' F-A-B-U-L-O-U-S."

The oven bell suddenly rang to let me know it was preheated. I left my spelling homework and returned to my cooking station to finish preparing the batter. I mixed in the flour, the eggs, the baking soda, and the vanilla, following Mimi's recipe exactly. Now, I needed to add in three cups of oats. I poured the oats into my measuring cup and measured out one cup.

"Moo!" I heard, bellowing loudly from the computer.

Isabella was IM'ing me on Dad's laptop. I dumped the oats into the mixing bowl, then went to the computer.

IzzyBELLA: Hey, chica! What's cookin'?
gOalgirl: My oatmeal cookies. Ha ha.
IzzyBELLA: LOL! U almost done?
gOalgirl: NO WAY!!!! Just started! Mom's busy.
Juliette—I mean JULES—at tennis. CANT
TALK NOW!!!
IzzyBELLA: OK. TTYL.

I lifted the oats container again. Had I put in one or two cups already? I couldn't remember. I studied the bowl. It looked as if I'd only put in one cup so far.

I measured out two more cups.

"One, two," I counted, pouring in the oats.

At that moment, the phone rang.

Ugh. I picked up the cordless phone and carried it over to where I'd been mixing.

"Hello?" I asked.

"Hi, Miss O." It was Harlie.

"Hey!" I said. "I can't talk!"

"Well that's a nice way to greet a friend!" Harlie joked.

"I'm sorry, Harl! But I'm kind of maxxed out at the moment! I'm trying to make the cookies, and do my homework and my book report at the same time!"

"Whoa! Can I help with anything?"

I let out a laugh. "Sure, you want to write my book report for me?"

"Ha, ha. No problem—if the Hinter Monster will like a book report on the latest X-Men comic!"

"I don't think so," I said. "Anyway, I really have to go."

"Okay, girlfriend. Let me know how it turns out."

"Thanks, Harlie. Bye!"

As I hung up, Dad was pulling on a sweatshirt and heading for the door. "I'm headed to pick up Juliette," he called to me. "When I get back, I'll help you with anything you need!"

I groaned. "Okay, Dad! But please hurry!"

I returned to my mixing bowl and stared inside. Had I put in the third cup of oats yet, or not? Dang! I couldn't remember.

"This really isn't going well," I mumbled out loud to myself. I tossed in another cup of oats and hoped for the best. As I mixed, I continued my spelling.

"Disastrous," I said. "As in, 'This night is turning disastrous.' D-I-S-A-S-T-R-O-U-S."

I finally finished preparing the cookie batter and I carefully mixed in some of the apple pieces Mom and I had baked the night before. I had to admit, the situation may have *looked* disastrous, but it was sure *smelling* good!

After spooning out the batter onto two big cookie sheets, I popped them into the oven. Now I could start typing up my book report as they baked. I set the oven timer and sat down at the laptop.

"*The Phantom Tollbooth*," I began to type, "by Norton Juster."

"For my first book report," I continued typing, "I read *The Phantom*

Tollbooth. It is the story of a boy named Milo and his watchdog named Tock." Thinking about Tock the Watchdog, I yawned and looked up at the kitchen clock.

9:13 p.m. It was going to be a long night.

I kept writing, trying to remember all the character's names from the story and thinking about interesting things to write about them. For this book report, I had to pick my three favorite characters and write about their personality traits. I couldn't remember the name of one of the characters, so I left the computer and headed upstairs to get my book.

As I leafed through the book, I heard my mother yell from downstairs.

"Olivia!" she cried. "The cookies!"

In a flash, I tossed the book onto my bed and raced down the stairs two steps at a time. When I got to the bottom, I could already smell the cookies burning. But the timer hadn't even rung.

My heart pounded in my chest as I yanked open the oven door. Using a mitt I pulled out the cookie trays as puffs of thick smoke poured out from the oven. Through the smoke I could see two dozen crispy black clumps sizzling on the trays.

My heart sank. The timer hadn't even rung yet. I gazed up to check the oven temperature. It read 450 degrees. I couldn't believe it!

"*Dad*!" I cried. "He set the oven to 450!"

I could see that Mom felt badly for me. "He's going to feel awful" she said. "I'm so, so sorry!"

I dumped the cookies into the trash and fell onto a kitchen stool. Tears welled up in my eyes. My mom came over and put her arms around me.

It was all so unfair.

Just then my dad and Juliette walked through the front door.

My dad took one look at me and knew I was upset. "Olivia? What's wrong?" he asked.

I barely made sense, trying to explain what had happened while holding back my tears. I sounded really pathetic. Anyway, Mom had to step in and explain everything.

"Oh, no! I am so sorry, honey!" Dad said.

I finally managed to take a few deep breaths to calm down.

"It's not all your fault," I choked. "I was just trying to do too many things at once. My book report, my homework, and baking the cookies."

"Well, how bad were the cookies burned?" Dad asked.

"Pretty bad," I said. "Can't you smell the smoke?"

Dad nodded. "Well, is there enough time to get another batch started?" he asked.

I looked at the clock. It was almost ten. Kind of late to be starting all over, but I really wanted to enter this contest.

"Yeah, I guess," I said, drying my eyes with my shirt collar.

"I can run out and get ingredients if you need them," Dad offered. "Or help you study. Whatever you need!"

I smiled. My family was the best. And I was just about to tell them that when I noticed Juliette was limping.

"Hel-lo?" she called out. "Did you forget about my foot?"

Dad spun around to my sister. "No, sweetie! Of course not!" He turned to Mom and me. "Juliette twisted her ankle on the tennis court," he said. "I promised I'd get her some aspirin and an ice pack and set her up comfortably in bed."

Juliette started limping toward the stairs and I gazed after her in disbelief. I mean, I'm sure her ankle hurt and all, but she hadn't said a word to me since coming inside! I was in the middle of a cookie catastrophe, and she barely even looked my way! Some sister!

In my mind, it was really the last straw. There was nothing I could do about her being my sister, but as far as I was concerned, Juliette was no longer my BFF.

Chapter 13
Trouble with a Capital Oatmeal

The next morning, though I hadn't gone to sleep until almost midnight the night before, I jumped out of bed filled with excitement. My cookies had turned out great—well, at least I *think* they'd turned out great. I'd wrapped them up immediately after they'd finished baking and I hadn't tasted them yet. They had certainly smelled great!

As soon as the cookies had turned golden brown, Mom and I had pulled them from the oven and wrapped them in foil, then in a zipper plastic bag. Mimi had taught us to do this while they were still piping hot, in order to keep them extra moist and chewy. I'd also found a pretty cookie platter to display them on—which I would do moments before the contest. I wanted to keep them sealed until the last possible second!

With the cookies complete, and my book report and homework finished as well, I was actually excited to get to school!

Dad drove me in early because I couldn't carry everything to school— my bag, the cookies, and the ingredients—by myself. And when he told me

Juliette was staying home today because of her ankle, I forced myself not to care. I didn't care what Juliette did or didn't do anymore. I still had three other BFFs out there. I wasn't going to waste my time thinking about somebody who never thought about me.

Dad was really a great help. I think he was still feeling guilty about the oven because he carried all my things when I got out of the car and he even walked me to my classroom. I was surprised—and a little relieved—to see that Mrs. Hintermeister wasn't in yet.

"Good luck, honey!" Dad said, as he planted a kiss on my forehead. "I really hope you win. You deserve it!"

After he left, I unpacked my books and reviewed my homework and my spelling words. The Hinter Monster walked into the classroom at a quarter to eight and gave me a nod.

"You're in early, Olivia," she said.

"I baked cookies for the contest," I told her. "And my father drove me in today because I had so much to carry."

Maybe I was still a little tired from the night before, or maybe I was still sleeping and this all was a dream, but I could swear I saw a smile on my teacher's face.

Unfortunately, it disappeared as quickly as it came.

"Very nice, Olivia," she said. "I didn't know you were entering the contest."

"I am," I said, sort of shocked that I was carrying on a semi-normal conversation with the Hinter Monster. "I love to bake."

"So do I," she said with a wink.

Okay, now I knew I was dreaming! The Hinter Monster had just winked at me!

Just then, other kids began filing into the classroom and the noise level rose. When the bell rang, everyone took their seats quickly. I noticed that of all the kids in my class, only one other had come to school with something to enter in the contest. Her name was Kaleigh Preto and she lived a few blocks from me.

"This morning, as you may already know," Mrs. Hintermeister said to the class, "we have an assembly."

Some kids cheered, until the Hinter Monster shot them a look.

"Along with the middle division, all classes from the lower division will be treated to a presentation from Sage School students who have chosen to enter the school's baking contest."

Again, kids cheered. I wondered if they were genuinely excited about watching the judging for a baking contest, or if they were just happy to be missing morning lessons.

Me, I was happy about both!

At 8:30 a.m., it was time for us to line up and head to the assembly. Carefully, I carried my cookies—which were still wrapped—and my cookie platter, and headed for the auditorium with my class. When we filed into the auditorium and found our seats, I looked around for the girls but I didn't see them.

"Our class will be first," Mrs. Hintermeister told us. "Olivia and Kaleigh, come with me. Everyone else, please remain in your seats. Miss Rumstein, one of the new student teachers, will remain with the class until I return."

Kaleigh and I followed Mrs. Hintermeister up onto the stage. While we waited in the wings, I carefully unwrapped a dozen of my cookies—they felt so moist and they smelled really great! I was sure they tasted delicious, too. I was tempted to try one, but I wanted the judges to have extra if they wanted more. Remembering how they had flown off the table at last year's bake sale, I was betting they'd *all* want seconds . . . even thirds!

I positioned the cookies on the cookie platter, trembling with excitement. The judges were going to be blown away!

As we stood in the wings waiting for all the classes from both divisions to file into the auditorium, I suddenly spotted Juliette in the center aisle of the auditorium. That was weird. What was she doing in school? Dad had said her ankle was pretty bad.

Juliette seemed to be in a heated discussion with one of the teachers from middle division. Was she upset? Were they arguing? I couldn't tell.

Not that I cared, mind you. It was just weird, that's all.

Anyway, I was still wondering as I watched her hobble over to another teacher. Again, she seemed anxious, waving her arms around as she spoke.

What was going on?

Just then, Principal Sack stepped up to the microphone and began the program. I decided not to pay attention to what my sister was doing and concentrate on the contest. Whatever it was probably had nothing to do with me, anyway.

When Principal Sack called my name, I stepped forward toward the judges' table. One of the judges smiled at me. "What have you baked for us?" she asked.

"These are called Miss O's Really Oatmealies," I said proudly. "Oatmeal cookies."

"Very nice!' the judge replied as I passed a cookie to each of the six judges. "Cute name, too!" she said.

I stood off to the side, next to Kaleigh, and I was beaming. Just wait until they tasted my cookies! They would probably declare me the winner on the spot!

As I watched the judges each put a cookie to their lips, from the corner of my eye I noticed Mrs. Hintermeister standing off to the side of the stage.

She was talking to Juliette!

Huh? What was going—

Before I could finish my thought, a strange sound came from the judges' table and distracted me. Was that . . . *a gag*?

I gulped anxiously as I saw all six judges frown in disgust! One judge actually spit my cookie on the floor!

The blood drained from my face. What was happening? Nobody had ever reacted so badly to my cookies before!

This was . . . DISASTROUS!

Chapter 14
AH! So That's the Way the Cookie Crumbles!

I was in such shock that I couldn't get a word out.

In a daze I watched as Mrs. Hintermeister and Juliette approached the judges' table and began whispering to the judges. All I could do was stand there and blink in confusion. At one point they all looked over at me—Mrs. Hintermeister, Juliette, and the judges—then they turned back and continued their whispering.

In the front row of the auditorium I noticed Isabella, Harlie, and Justine staring up at me. I shrugged to let them know I had no idea what was going on. No idea why Juliette was in school and talking with Mrs. Hintermeister. No idea why the judges had gagged on my cookies. And no idea what was going to happen next.

What *did* happen next was that Juliette came limping toward me, holding something in the crook of her arm that *seemed* vaguely familiar—

Our blue sugar container? The one from home, that had been so hard to find last night? I scrunched up my nose in confusion. What was she doing with *that*? And hadn't I brought that to school with me this morning?

Mrs. Hintermeister followed my sister and soon they were standing right in front of me.

"Do you have your ingredients with you?" Mrs. Hintermeister asked me.

I nodded, wishing somebody would let me in on what was happening! "Yes," I whispered to her. "I have the ingredients back in the classroom." I had taken everything to school with me, since as part of the rules the winner would have to actually bake their winning recipe for the judges. I was about ask Juliette how she was holding the same blue sugar container that I had remembered bringing to school this morning, but before I could speak, Mrs. Hintermeister gave me a gentle nudge.

"Then go get them!" she ordered. "And meet us in the cafeteria!"

In the cafeteria? "But—"

Before I could finish, Mrs. Hintermeister and Juliette headed off the stage. My teacher helped Juliette down the stairs and I watched as Juliette whispered to Isabella, Justine, and Harlie. Then all of them left the auditorium together.

Well, there was no doubt about it now, I thought, watching the group of them leave together. I must still be asleep because this was all just so unreal!

"Wake up!" I ordered myself.

When I arrived at the cafeteria, Mrs. Hintermeister was there waiting for me, along with Juliette, Isabella, Justine, and Harlie. Everything was happening so fast, I didn't have time to think straight! If I *had*, I might have thought about how weird it was for my teacher to be hanging out in the cafeteria with my sister and my three best friends.

"Miss O!" Juliette cried. She was sitting on a cafeteria chair with her foot up on another chair. She was still holding our sugar container.

"I wish someone would tell me what was going on!" I said helplessly. "And what you're doing with that," I added, pointing to the blue container.

Juliette managed to stand up and limp over to where I was standing. "Miss O!" she said. "*This* is the sugar! From our pantry. I used it on my apple crêpes the other night because I think Mimi never makes stuff sweet enough. Anyway, I'd accidentally put it back in the wrong cabinet.

I looked at her as if she were nuts. "Yeah? So?"

"Well, I didn't think about it until this morning, after you left for school, when I needed it for my cereal. I took it from where I had put it the other night and as I was eating, I started wondering if you had known where it was last night when you were baking."

I rubbed my eyes. "Juliette, what are you talking about?" I asked.

"You used the salt in your cookies last night, instead of the sugar! The salt was in the exact same blue plastic container." Juliette frowned sympathetically.

I gasped in horror.

"Oh, no! I can't believe it!" I pulled the blue container from my bag of ingredients and opened the lid. I dipped my finger in and tasted it.

"Yuck! It *is* salt!"

Mrs. Hintermeister stepped toward me. "I had a feeling something wasn't right," she said. "So after Juliette told me about the mix-up, I spoke with the judges and was able to convince them to let you have another chance."

I looked at the others, then back at my teacher. "R-R-Really?" I stammered. The Hinter Monster had done that for *me*?

Mrs. Hintermeister smiled. "Yes, Olivia. When your sister explained what had happened, I knew your chances at winning were over. And from what I remember about your oatmeal cookies from the soccer fundraiser last year, I think you deserve another shot! They were quite exceptional!"

Mrs. Hintermeister looks so different when she's smiling, you have no idea.

I turned to Juliette. "So you came to school with a bad ankle just to help me?" I asked "I'm kind of surprised. Lately you've been so, well, so you-know-what to me."

Juliette frowned. "I know, Miss O," she said. "And you can say it—what I've been lately. A real horror. The worst sister ever. And the worst friend," she added, looking over at the girls.

"When I saw your face last night,"she continued, "after the cookies burned, it made me realize that it wasn't just me going through rough stuff in the new school year. We are all going through stuff. I felt so badly for the way I've been acting that I wanted to make it up to you."

"Really?" I asked in amazement. "But you just went upstairs last night and didn't even help me," I pointed out.

"My ankle was really killing me," she said. "I couldn't help you in the kitchen, or with your homework," adding, with a quick look at Mrs. Hintermeister, "because that would be *wrong*. But I realized I could help you with that *other* thing you've been asking me about."

My eyes narrowed. I wasn't following.

"So I went online to research that *other* stuff you needed, and look at what I found!"

I swallowed hard as Juliette handed me a printout of an article she'd found online. It was about Mrs. Hintermeister! Yikes! Was she nuts? The Hinter Monster was standing right next to her!

I must have looked incredibly panicked because Mrs. Hintermeister said, "It's okay, Olivia. Juliette already showed me what she found. And it's all true."

All true? I thought with disbelief. *The chalk…jail . . . all of it?*

I grabbed the paper from Juliette and stared at the words on the page. When I read what it said, I had to stop myself from laughing out loud.

"So you thought I'd been in jail?" Mrs. Hintermeister asked.

I turned to my teacher, relieved to see that she was grinning.

"Yes. Well, kind of," I admitted, feeling a bit embarrassed. "I mean, we did see a picture of you that said you had been behind bars."

Juliette let out a laugh. "When that picture caption said 'Local Teacher Behind Bars,' it meant behind Magic Cookie Bars! I discovered Mrs. Hintermeister and her husband are the owners of AH! Baked Goods Company. AH! stands for Applegate and Hintermeister!"

"You see, Olivia," Mrs. Hintermeister went on, "I won a baking contest very similar to this contest many years ago. I entered my own original recipe for Magic AppleMeister Cookie Bars . . . and I won! The cookie bars went on to be sold all over the world, and my husband and I eventually bought the company and changed the name to AH! Baked Goods! So I know how important this contest is to you, too."

"Wow, you invented Magic AppleMeister Cookie Bars." Harlie exclaimed. "I love those!"

It was all too much to comprehend. My sister had gone through so much trouble—hobbling around school in pain—just for me. And my teacher was *not*, after all, a convicted felon. She was a famous bakery owner who had dreamed up an award–winning recipe for cookies!

"Believe it or not, I feel partially responsible for your sugar/salt mistake," Mrs. Hintermeister said. "I've really overworked you and the other students. I'm sure it's been a bit overwhelming for you."

I nodded. *You have no idea,* I thought.

"I also happen to know that many students at the Sage School think I'm a very strict teacher," she went on. "Mean, even."

I stared down at the floor. What could I say to her? "Oh, yes, you're the meanest teacher on the planet and we call you the Hinter Monster?" I don't think so.

Mrs. Hintermeister sighed. "I suppose I am strict," she went on. "But I'm a firm believer in following rules. I've learned that students respond better to a strict teacher. They work harder and they care more about their work.

"The harder I work my students," she added, "the better they seem to do in class. In fact, every year my students have the best test scores," she told us. "One hundred percent of my students maintain a B average or better! I think that's pretty terrific! So if I'm a little more strict than the other teachers . . . "

"*A little?*" I joked.

Juliette nudged me.

"Just kidding," I added sheepishly.

Mrs. Hintermeister smiled. "That's okay," she said.

"But what about all those kids that you left back?" Harlie asked her.

Sheesh! Leave it to Harlie to ask something like that!

Mrs. Hintermeister laughed out loud, which surprised us all. "Tell me," she said. "Do you all believe every rumor you hear?" she asked. "What about the one about how I threw something at a student?" she asked.

"Chalk," Harlie reminded her.

"Yes, chalk. Did you hear that one, too?"

My eyes widened as I nodded.

"So silly," Mrs. Hintermeister said.

"I *knew* it wasn't true!" Harlie exclaimed knowingly.

I made a face at her.

"They are all rumors," Mrs. Hintermeister confirmed. "Every last one. Well, except for the stories about me being strict. Those are true! And I'm not going to lighten up on you now, Olivia, just because I enjoy your cookies!"

"Oh, that's—"

Mrs. Hintermeister grinned. "I'm just kidding," she said. "I suppose I *can* lighten up," she said. "But just a little," she added. "After all, I don't want any of my students slacking off this year. Especially one of my most promising students!"

I brightened. "Really?" I asked.

"Absolutely," my teacher replied.

"How about me . . . am I forgiven?" Juliette asked, her eyes wide as saucers.

It took me just a half a second to decide. I mean, this was *Juliette, my sister*. She would always be my BFF—no matter what. "Of course I forgive you!" I said hugging her. We were having a dorky sister moment until I remembered everyone else standing there, and then we just started giggling.

"And now," Mrs. Hintermeister said, smiling as she herded us into the school kitchen, "it's time to get to work and help Olivia whip up a batch of cookies those judges can really sink their teeth into!"

We watched in amazement as she began pulling out mixing bowls and measuring cups and spoons. It was unbelievable. My teacher—the inventor of the Magic Cookie Bars!

"This is just all so . . .*cool*!" I said as we worked together mixing and measuring.

"Don't you mean *fabulous*?" Isabella joked, using one of my spelling words.

I laughed. "Okay, it's all so F-A-B-U-L-O-U-S!" I said.

Mrs. Hintermeister laughed, too. It was a sound I could really get used to!

So yes, it was true. I was actually *liking* the Hinter Monster today. Having seen this whole other side to her and all.

And who knew? Even if I didn't win *this* baking contest, maybe I'd still have a career in baked goods someday.

If only I could manage to stay OUT of trouble and ON the Hinter Monster's good side!